About the Author

Clare Dunn grew up in the foothill suburbs of Perth Australia - the most isolated capital city in the world. She attended school locally and was a keen sports person. She traveled at a young age with her family to the UK and Ireland. The search for adventure and passion for creativity blossomed. She moved to Bunbury for love for her now wife, Ellie. She writes, runs an online business of Creative Development and travels the world in search of wild adventure.

www.claredunn.com.au

A Sea Of Troubles

Clare Dunn

Muse Books

Part 1: The Ship

1. Celine

'Will the belly of this ship hold me forever?' The question I pose to myself. Water swirls around my feet and stinks so bad. Mould grows on the lower beams, submerged for months. We haven't stopped for long enough at a port to get it fixed. No time; that's what the bosses say, above. This is the way the world works. We hit a rather big wave and my semi-dry shins are sloshed with water.

'Well, semi-dry no longer,' I say to myself. This won't dry and will be damp all night. I am so wrinkly my skin might fall off. I hear footsteps clonking down the galley stairs.

'Hey, you!' I hear thrown my way. It's as if I don't have a name, or it's too hard to remember. Us women all look alike, don't you know? A clam shell between our legs and a mouth that could run all day. It seems this is the opinion of a lot of the crewmen. Specifically men. I smirk and answer in my best good girl voice, 'Yes, Captain!'

'You bloody wrench, I've told you not to call me that. If the real captain hears you, I'll be strung out on the deck like a fish sunbaking for a week. Now git your slimy fins up on deck and give it a good old wash.'

Inwardly, I cringe. The knife I feel to my heart hurts deeply when they give me jobs like this. I'm reminded of the status and capabilities thrust upon me. But what choice do I have? It's what good girls do. What all girls do and are good for. The labour assigned to us: Wash, cook, clean. Tend to the accessories of the men. Always the assistant, second to a master, no guide and no navigation point. Always telling us where to go, when and how far we should jump. Before we 'hurt' ourselves. It's like we only have half a brain. The rest just takes up space in our heads, or else they'll cave in. That's what I hear them tell me. Then I argue, talk back and stutter. I don't even own my own words; stuck in me like I'm stuck on this boat, going nowhere but around and around in a sea of hopes and dreams. My back hunches. I drag my bucket and mop to the stairs. Each one is a reminder of the steps I take daily to remain in the same place I always am.

Attached to the life, I am. To the pain. It's all I know; to go outside of it would be to die. At least here I am alive... Barely. Breathing pains my chest. Not because of the salt or the tar fumes etching their stench and acrid acid onto my lungs. The pain comes from my heart. That this—my waste of a life—is what I've been spending the space in my heart doing. I might die at any moment on these ships at sea. Go down to the whales and fish and never return. That is the possibility every moment of every day. And this is my fate... Or so I've been thinking. Part of me knows that outside of this, there is more. More to me. More to life. And to live that would be to be free. To join the dolphins dancing over, under and through the waves. Surf spray no bother, but play. That's what it's like to be free and when part of you knows there is more to this, more to what I see in front of me now. I can't help but hurt to choose this day in 'n out. Footsteps approach.

'Git your slimy sea legs up on deck,' I hear him yell, shouting down through the hatch at the young ones. New hands that need teaching about what goes on on deck. They need to be shown the way, how things are done around here. How it all works. How our world revolves.

Swish swish; the sound of the wind rolls through the sails. Here we are again. Same-same, but a sliver of change. A day broken by the silence of sadness on repeat. My heart aches. It's like standing behind a barrier to the world. One where the world exists outside of me. Playing out like a vision in front of me. Separate. And here I stand in my own little world, or a big world of emptiness. Exposed in my loneliness: bare, naked and vulnerable. Broken and useless for the world to see. A shadow of what others exist as.

BAM. The head hits the deck in front of me, jolting me out of the stupor I was wallowing in.

'Hey! Grab that useless garbage and follow me below deck,' she yells at me. I pick up the severed grey blob of a head rolling gently in front of me. I'm broken from my trance of sadness and nothingness, like the crack of movement breaks the silence of the day.

'Woah,' I think. 'That was a deep hole I was in. Where would I go? How far would I sink into the darkness of my own mind if the world didn't turn around me?'

Back and forth, the days melt into one. The same roller coaster rise and fall. Deep darkness. Hollow reality. Back and forth in my heart, its strings pulled to its tethered edges. Hanging on and hanging around. Who would care if I ended up like this head too?

Blood trickles behind me as I trail below deck. It's extra salty here. The sound of the waves lapping against the sides soothes the pain that I can feel down here. These souls yearn for life but are stuck here, kept captive by death. That's my job here: to keep souls. We track them. We take them and we hold their life until it runs into us. Leaking out at the edges to be sucked up by the pitiful existence of all around me: the needy, the despairing, the heartless. The rats down here keep us all down. We hold each other down, bonded together over pain and knowing that we are all craving the same thing: A heart. A beat that we can live by that guides us and shows us the way to freedom and happiness and the deep intimate connection that we so crave. The pull of our souls, now the souls we enslave, calling us home.

Pacing the deck; that is how I see her today. Grumpy as always, a smile for no one, woman or man alike. Catching her eye, I just as quickly turn away as her stare pierces my heart, my soul. A cold and warm chill runs down my back. Switching temperatures. I feel her eyes linger on me, assessing, gauging, watching. The uncomfortable feeling grows and I feel myself move my body away, behind the rigging, to trigger some sort of release from me. Get her away from making me feel uncomfortable. Just as soon as I've relaxed, two boots stomp down in front of me on the deck.

'Oi, what are you looking at, wretch?' I hear. 'You think you have the right, you have the audacity to look at me? Staring and judging with those eyes I saw. Go on, enlighten us with what you know. Regale us with your handy way with words.'

She's practically on top of me now and as much as I want to hide, melt into the deck boards, I know it's a useless hope. What comes next is easily every bit as detrimental as my actions this morning and for the life of me I can't imagine what's going through my head as I say it.

'You look sad, Ma'am. Like you wanted more from your life and this is where you've ended up. Alone in a sea of people. In a position of perceived power but feeling every bit as out of control in your life as the "scum" you refer to us as.' As soon as the words leave my mouth I'm shocked. Not as shocked as Daone. The look on her face is priceless... But that's something I'll enjoy later. Right now I'm in fear for my life, and my face is the closest thing to her boot. Just a short extension and I'm all exposed. And that's exactly what happens. I feel the cartilage snap and warm blood congeal and flow down my face. I recoil, as much from shock as pain. What I said didn't come from malice but an innocent answer to a question.

2. Daone

I feel the cold breeze and salt on my face, my skin almost burning with the spray. I kind of like it. The pain I put myself in to look into the wind and stare into the eye of the storm. Fear rises in my chest and I let it sit there, feeling it all and feeling nothing. Empty and taking in what's in the moment. Here, I let the earth hit me with its juggernaut of energy. It makes me feel small. It makes me feel alive. Something has to, these days. It's not me. A part of me is gone. Missing. I remember the shadow of its feeling: spirited and alive. Thriving. What is that? What does that feel like? To have words at my disposal but never having the need to use them. What's the point in having a huge vocabulary when all you can flex is describing another's world? To never speak words like love, excitement, joy, discovery, in my own story. To describe how I'm feeling. Always to look in at another world from the outside and wish to know how it feels. I stare off into the distance and wish, yearn, for something different. Something more.

Fast, that is how we are going. Fast in a bad way. Going down fast. Spinning and turning and diving. Below the waves, it feels. Crashing over me. Down, down, always down, into my heart and going nowhere fast.

'Hey are you okay?' It's been so long since anyone has asked, since anyone has cared how I feel, that I blank and tune out. Fear wells up inside me. I don't know what to say besides the standard, 'Good,' and even then it seems too much. Too vulnerable, like acknowledging that I have feelings makes me human, makes me weak. But here we are. Crazy, when it's so obvious that we are skin, bones and emotion.

3. Celine

White noise, crackling in my ears, fuzzing in my brain. The groggy feelings engulf me. I can taste the acid in my throat and the dryness on the top of my mouth. The bottom has gone out of my stomach. I open my eyes and look around in the dark. I can feel the roll of the ship so I know I am still in this hell hole. I must be in the tally.

What happened? I manage to form a coherent thought to ask myself. Strange that. That I actually think about stuff first and don't just say the first thing that pops into my head. Well, sometimes. When it doesn't really matter as there is no one around me now who I can piss off. It comes back to me now. The incident up on deck. I scold myself for speaking so freely. I know better. I shove down the freedom I naturally have with shame, reminding myself for next time that that is not how to act. *That is not how to act.* Repeating it over and over in my head. Replaying the scenario until I can almost convince myself it has happened differently. Preparing myself for next time. Next time

I have an urge to be wild. To be myself, that's not okay to be. That's how you get beaten. Shoved down in the dark and forgotten. That's how you die.

4. Daone

I don't remember the last time I slept well. I remember I used to, as a child... or did I? Did I just feel less stressed? Less under the weather, everyday? More excited about life that it kept me engaged during the day? Or were my days more centred around rest when I needed it? All these helpful thoughts that go through my head during the night, when I'm meant to be sleeping. The time I have allocated to sleeping. Who decided this for me? Someone outside of myself. The collective.

'This is when you shall sleep. If you don't sleep during your allocated time, no more time will be allocated to you.' No leniency. No flexibility. No flow for me, or anyone it seems, once you reach a certain age. You are initiated into adulthood by being told what you can do. What your limitations are, where you belong. What an initiation. What a life. Weird. I haven't thought like this. I just followed the road in front of me and this is where I ended up. Thirty, alone on a ship of strangers I loath. Weird. I've never admitted that to myself before. I've felt it. I know that much. This feeling isn't new for me, I just never knew what it stood for, before. What's making me make this connection now? What have I done differ—... I instantly think of the morning. When I split that wretched woman's face down on deck. But why should that matter? Why should it take up brain space? Why should it take up *my* heart space? This confusion unsettles me. Something unknown outside of myself. I have the control. I know me and the *whys* of the world. Of my world. This peasant should not be taking up this space, keeping me awake. If she gives me the reason, I'll make sure she knows what a worthless piece of shit she really is. Yesterday will feel like a teddy bear's hug compared to the beating I'll serve up to her. I roll over and settle to go back to sleep. I'm the wo'MAN. I've got this and I'll show them.

5. CELINE

Whispers ring in the dark. Voices. Shallow. Low. A hum of energy. Rippling through the dark. Ripping it. Ripping into the silence. Tearing at my ear. Tearing me awake. Pulling me from my sleep .The calm of my mind. The calm of being connected to the other side. The warmth. Avoidance of sleep. Like there is a chance this isn't real and my dream state is the real state. The world into which I am plunged is the fake one. The nightmare. This is how it feels sometimes... Voices. I can hear them. Catching snippets of sounds. Turning those sounds into words in my head.

'... you think she will come back...?'

'... you think she will make it ...?' The wondering hangs in the silence like glue. Sticky. It sticks to my heart. I take on what they are saying and attach it to my heart. It's in this moment and time I know they are talking about me. This is about me. Where am I going? Who is taking me there? Why wouldn't I come back? What? What? What? I get so overwhelmed my heart beats out of my chest. My brain can't even ask, 'What,' coherently. All I can do is be in my heart. Which is outside of my chest. The fear is so real, I wonder, is this what a heart attack feels like? Is this what beats me? My own body, turning against me. Me, unable to control every ounce of myself into being alive, into bending to my will. And then it stops. A slow beat is all that remains. My heart. Regulated. Beating normally. In this moment, I realise it's over. I'm back to being me. The anxiety sits just below the surface. A constant pal to me, taking it everywhere with me.

I am fully awake now. I can still hear the voices. They are just background noise. I turn away, disinterested, and take stock of my cell. A single mattress sits just off the ground. Covered in a dull, once-was-white sheet. I wonder if it would be cleaner to just sleep on the ground. It probably gets washed more. When the slime gets too much, when the water from the deck gets washed down, over the rotting wooden beams that make up the floor. It's easier to just let them rot than change them. That way you don't have to move people around too much. You can spend the resources on the upper levels, keeping them clean, letting anyone below you live in a little more dust, decay and filth than you. I'm sure the dirt gets between the cracks in the floor so we are actually living in the filth of the man who lives on top of us. A single metal bucket sits in the corner. Drinking water by morning, shitter in the evening. Better hope your body bends to the appointments of the day. Your problem if it doesn't. Am I selling this to myself? Am I convincing myself this is the way things are? Will always be? This is the world I live in. This is my hell. Some days I wonder why I wake up.

'The courage,' I hear a voice inside of myself say. The courage everyday to get up and hope that things will be better. To know it's hell and still wake up means you either like hell (if it's hell, why would I?) or you get up each day with the courage to live in that hell and create outside of it. To create something new.

6. Celine

I feel the sway of the boat side to side. It rattles my head and swishes what little I have in my stomach from side to side, reminding me how hungry I am. I hear footsteps coming on wood. The rattle of keys on a chain. Big old keys on a big old hook, clanking together. Not a huge set, just a few. My attention to this detail surprises me. The normal sound is chunky, heavy. It gives off the tell-tale sign of the key master, the guard coming to check on us participants in the cells. To dish out food with the cook, or to release someone back onto deck for duty—usually with a guard, in case the captives get touchy about being locked up for so long, now free. This is different. I cock my head to one side, keeping my eyes closed. Wanting to pick up on as much information as possible without giving away too much. Don't want to seem too smart around here. That just gets things worse. The more valuable you are the more you can be used for that skill set, that gift. Bled dry, I've seen people with gifts become. Melted away in the sun. To nothing. To death. To a fate worse than death. Alive but empty. A void moving through life. Seeing life but never being able to touch it. Shadows of their former heart.

This old man, the key master, he has many tasks but his most important defines him and lends to his name. The master of the keys. Granting freedom or solitude. The breath of fresh air or the stench of secondhand air, breathed in by the pitiless souls of those too scared or cowardly to live a proper life, who end up here. In the depth of this death ship. The wood, stained black.

The tales of how it came about is that a fire tried to burn the ship but even that light would not be suffered here. It could not exist and so the decks remained whole and all the remnants of the fire were the black coloured ship that sailed.

The key master and his henchman (a smaller man who hunched over and followed him around) ead me up the stairs. It feels like an age going up them. There is no effort to spare my limbs from smashing into each one as I'm half carried, half pushed up them. The sunlight touches my eyes and burns, blinding me. My head lolls as the intense light and weight of the week spent under deck catches what little energy I have and drains it. All I see is light, until the dark engulfs me.

7. Daone

The next part. This is the next part. I know I'm in a new stage of my life. *My life.* What an odd thought to have. Of course it's my life. Then why don't I feel like it most of the time? I don't remember being aware of the responsibilities of my life. Having an awareness of my world around me. What is going on around me? Water. Always water. Solid ground is a thing of the past. This is my life now, on the water. It's a privilege to step on dry land. That's how it's always been. A world without, is my world. No ground under my feet. I sometimes imagine what it would be like to step on the earth and feel its energy. I can feel the ocean. It's cold and wet and sucking of life force. It takes your warmth. It takes the dry. It washes away the feelings of stability and connection. A world of unease, emotions of despair and of sorrow, for we do not know what dwells beneath our feet. I think we feel that. The unknown, always changing below us and it causes us to act differently to how we normally would. I can't even say why I know that, but I do. That this isn't 'normal.' That there is a 'normal,' a feeling of home in my heart and we don't have it. I don't see it in the people around me. I don't feel it in their actions and their words. I don't feel them share their heart with the world and I feel mine shrivelling up inside of my chest when I don't share, express, be in the world. This is the effect the water has on us.

I say us. It's one of the only times I feel a part of something. A part of a team. It just happens that this team is Team Fuck Up: what we are doing to ourselves, what we are doing to the world. One day at a time, further away from our core. One terrible idea hatching at a time. Closer to a death fate for us and the planet, yet still I have a hope. It's a flutter in my chest that makes me stop. Makes me wonder. No, I *choose* to listen too. I wonder if all around me people feel the same and choose not to stop? They're choosing not to listen and that choice is why we are here in the first place. Too many people choosing not to listen to the heart inside all of us.

8. Celine

I look up. The white light blinds me. Voices swirl around my head. The crew are walking past me on the deck, rags hanging off their bodies, eyes hollow in the light. The sun is showing, hiding nothing. Pale faces staring back at me or floating aimlessly across the deck, caught in another's plan. Pulled along by something outside of themselves. A current flowing towards someone else's goal. Someone else's hollow goal of greed, pain and fear. Footsteps tap the deck. I can hear the sails catch the wind, holding it momentarily then passing it into the breeze. It's like holding power for a moment only to have it slip away and onwards, to a new fate. It's something I wish I could harness; my own power. Feelings like this keep coming up. I see it in the world around me. I'm starting to notice, to see the world in a different way and... feel. Feel the pain I am in and... feel more, I hope. What I imagine *better* feels like. Feeling like I don't want to be here right now, if there is a way out. A way of ending it all and feeling nothing. Or a long hard slog out of this reality, to a better one. Thoughts of the day.

Feelings of the moment. Thought notes to myself. I head back below deck. Even the depths pull at me when surrounded by this much pain and suffering. They will take me below again soon anyway. I may as well take myself and fool myself into thinking it was my decision and not an inevitability of the situation. I am followed, the keys swinging and jangling down the steps after me. As the lock clicks shut on my brief soiree, I retreat into my own heart and examine my life from the position I am in today. Dark and dank creeps into my head. Always closing in, always closing in.

9. Daone

Hey, today I feel happy! That doesn't happen much. Doesn't happen everyday. But here we are. Oh wait, maybe it's not happiness. Maybe I'm blasé. I don't care. Very different. A very different feeling. Hmmm. Well, there you go. Another day, another idiot. Yep that's how my day is going to go. I can feel it. We're standing on the deck. 'We' being my loser assistant Gerald and myself. Bubbly, enthusiastic me. I don't turn up to work ecstatic everyday and today is not one of those days, nor any other day. I walk across to the opposite side of the bridge and lose the sense of closeness with another for a brief moment. Right behind, Gerald is moving, shadowing me. He is either watching me or feels a sense of safety following someone superior to him. That way, he can't get in trouble. He is always on hand, in my footsteps. An adequate worker. We keep this up for a while. I move away and gain a sense of isolation. A sense of sovereignty, only to have it plucked away from me by my smelly Gerald cocoon. That's how it feels. A cocoon wrapping tighter around my body. Tighter around my soul, as if I am aware of my soul. What a useless skill. What a useless endeavour. It always has been.

When I was younger I was told, 'Useless, dangerous.' It almost cost me this placement. This 'good' job, on this ship filled with hopeless souls. Going nowhere but always on the move. It's been nine years of this hell, sailing the world. My world. I've come here, to exist here on this hell ship. I just feel so over this. IT! The life I feel I have only known because of how long it has gone on. Gerald moves into my space once more and it tips me over the edge.

'FOR FUCK'S SAKE, GERALD!' I explode. Gerald doesn't know what to do. His body and mind go into overdrive. The fear is taking over, taking the reins and operating for him. I see the cogs turn behind his eyes. One... two... three seconds pass and Gerald is frozen on the spot. *Maybe if I don't move, she can't see me?* I bet that's what he is thinking. Pathetic. Yet I feel sorry for him. Am I not in a similar response across my life? If I don't move, maybe the forces that be won't see me, won't notice that I'm not like the rest. That I feel. That I am aware. That I crave a life outside of this one with... dare I think it... Love. Purpose. A sense of belonging for who I am and not who others want me to be. I think all this in the split seconds I'm watching the pathetic, smelly Gerald. I wonder if he would choose to smell like fish if he knew how bad it was. Does his lack of awareness of this hell hole permeate over to the awareness of his stench?

'GET THE FUCK OUT OF HERE!' I yell again. Partly to calm myself by doing something and partly to alleviate the pure panic and terror I see before me and that cannot be soothed by me. Better he be away and neither of us have to deal with it. His quick footsteps echo and recede below deck. I am left alone. Cold with the spray and salt, catching the skin on my face before being dried by the wind. A crispy layer left behind. Salty. Just like me.

10. Daone

I dream. I see the ship from above; a grand master of the sea. Huge sails flap in the wind and rain and salt. Grand, like nothing we have ever seen before. Where we come from is green, like the sea. Mossy and cold. Drenched in the clear rain that mingles around the feet of our ship, if it did indeed have feet. Slipping through the sea, brushing it aside with each movement. I reflect on how funny it is, how you can see something as big as a ship and wonder if it's moving at all. When there are no markings, nothing to go by. Are we moving at all or are we just standing still, with the sea moving around us, at anchor in the open ocean? Impossible in my mind. A possibility though when I am outside of myself. Outside of my limitations and structures. When my world isn't dictated to me but created by me. I am changed. I feel different. A different person. Even my clothes look different. Am I still Daone, the salty sea dog who beat that girl on deck? I wake.

11. Celine

It's cold, so cold and so dark. Water is still dripping from the ceiling.

As if they never fixed this. It's not that hard, I think to myself. Anger wells up inside me. How can I be treated like this? I'm a person. A living, breathing miracle. We all are and this is how we treat each other. Keeping us locked up, working us like slaves. Taking away our dignity and our basic rights to exist. Even that gets taken away. Our lives; the ultimate steal. To take that from someone... For what gain? Greed. Greed has brought us here. Greed in our hearts, believing that we need more. More of all the niceties in the world. And you have to step on others to get it. I am so annoyed. So furious. That that woman can take from me. It hurts my heart and I shut off to it and tune in to the pain. Pain and anger go hand in hand. One gets easier the stronger the other gets. They are linked, feeding off each other.

I simmer in the pit of a ship that takes me nowhere but deeper into my own hell. We may as well be standing still. It would be better for me as I'd at least not be closer to death and that is all that awaits me here. A prisoner of my own selfish need to have desires, wants, needs in life, dictated by me. That is what has brought me here. My choice to join in. To be more and go after more. I don't know how it all went so wrong. What I set out for and where I've ended up are worlds apart from each other. Have I changed? Am I different, so I changed the directory of my life? I thought I'd set out to be free, to adventure and see the world. What went so wrong that this is where I am? Alone with my thoughts, I shake. I hate the cold and the cold loves me. Enveloping me in its chill, I slip into thought sleep. That's what I call it when my brain doesn't shut off but I am not in my body. A limbo where I exist in my thoughts only. Paralysed by my own pool of dreams. Dreams and nightmares. Where are we going tonight?

12. The Collision

A loud bang wakes the ship. The occupants start spilling out onto the deck like rats. Some seek to jump overboard straight away, sealing the fate of the ship without a fight. Less hands mean less help onboard. Others helplessly struggle with the ropes that bind the sails. Unfurling and furling, altering where the wind catches and sails through. They are intent on fighting until the end, a 'not over until it's over' type of people. Some will be washed away with the waves. Others choose to go down with the ship. Martyrs, thinking they can save the mother. Daone walks out onto deck, taking all this in, knowing she is getting off the ship. She has no allegiances with the darkness that put her here. Her own path is hers to walk, even if it is a struggle. Something stops her as she carries the rations she has gathered to the dingy strapped to the back of the ship. Stowed for emergencies. Sometimes smaller is better. A pang of guilt in her chest. What is this? She can't help thinking about the girl trapped below deck. Beaten by her earlier that week. For nothing more than looking at her the wrong way. Knowing her fate is sealed, unless she intervenes with action. But why would she do that? She doesn't know and in the end gives in to this feeling and moves anyway. Hoping somehow the small vessel remains tucked away, concealed by the dark tarp she slides back over it.

PART 2: CARNAGE

13. Celine

Whispers in the dark, that's all that Celine could hear. Shrieks fill the space where footsteps hit the stairs. Panic was rising. The space filled with an air of fear. Desperation hung thickly, being sucked and regurgitated with the foul energy of those about to die. All the hate, all the pain, all the darkness bubbled up to the surface as bodies sensed their time coming to a close. An end. Quiet in her mind. She could feel at peace.

Celine knew she wasn't going to die today. She didn't know why or how but it was a quiet feeling that she watched the empty space with. Steps, those steps. Could they be coming for her? Was this her next step out of here? Curiously, she angled her body in the cell so she could get as early a look at the new occupant of the space as possible. Wide shoulders. Tall head. She walked out of the doom and dark and stepped up to the cell.

'We're getting out of here,' she said. The information was easy for Celine to take in. It made sense to her. But it sent the rest of the room into a frenzy. The awareness that they would most likely die and there was someone getting out right in front of them worked the energy to what felt like a breaking point. The point where you wonder if steel could be bent by human hands. If they struggled hard enough, could they get out?

'What about the others?' Celine asked, as this woman who'd only recently beat her for looking back actually saw her, and unlocked her door.

'They will kill you, and they will definitely kill me.' She said this as a matter of fact. Not laced with any hate or sympathy. Just that it is what it is. Inside, Celine knew this was the case. She just felt, just hoped there was a chance. That things could be different. She nodded and followed past the screaming masses, up and up, and listened to the woman speak.

'All that awaits them above deck is the cold sting of the ocean. Without supplies they will turn on each other and become the animals they are here now.' The words hurt Celine. She knew there was good inside all, but she also knew it was true though. She could feel it. She had been there with them. In the dark. Inside and out. She gasped as her head hit the air above deck.

14. DAONE

Whispers in the dark, all around her, as she stepped through the space below the world she lived in. Below deck. She didn't come down here much, it reminded her of the places deep within her that were cold, dark and cruel. She didn't need that much help. Coming down there put her in a state. She put up walls. She blocked everyone out. She was a shell, a machine, hollow and performing the task set out down there: Release the woman from the deck, get out. It was plain and simple. She even had the keys ready so they'd only make a sound when she reached the door and slipped it into the lock. The space erupted when she did. All around her the noise was deafening. It overwhelmed her and she shrank more into herself, barely registering that she was talking but hearing words come from her mouth. They moved out and walked up onto the deck. Daone shook a little as she reached the cool air. Not because she was cold but to clear her energy. Bring her back to herself. Even then, it felt like the time spent below was a dream. Almost like she was knocked out, blacked out and sleepwalking the whole time. She felt like it was safe to come back to herself now. Open up and be tender, almost.

She hurried to the back deck and checked on the boat. It was still there and she relaxed a little more and got set, ready for departing. It was strange, the woman she had just saved was just standing there, looking at her. She couldn't read her expression. What was it? Confusion? Was she so dumb? They had to get going, the ship was sinking. Those able and willing to depart had done so and those unable and determined to stay had jobs to keep them busy. It was just the two of them back there. Her own sense of urgency was not met, not shared.

'Come on!' she urged, trying to instill some sense of urgency in her.

'Why did you save me?' Daone heard her speak and instantly wanted to hit her in the face again. Wanted to beat her and tell her she was stupid and not worth saving. Daone paused and then continued prepping the supplies, thinking she could force the situation into her control without violence.

'Why did you save me?' She heard the same words again. This time she crumbled under them. Her armour came down. Unable to hide, not wanting to become the person capable of committing such violence.

'I don't know.' The pain in the lie hurt more than the face she lost by not having a good reason in front of this... peasant, this low life sea dog.

'Why?' she asked again.

'Look, can we just leave?' Daone answered. 'Knowing won't change that in less than five minutes it won't be for anything and we will both die.' Celine took this in, didn't look happy about it, but gave a slight nod and helped Daone with the dingy. They had to lift it over the lip of the boat and while it hung suspended in the air, they both jumped in, lowering themselves with the rope and pulley into the choppy sea.

'What happened to the boat?' the woman asked. Daone replied as she looked back at her home of the past being swallowed by the sea.

'We hit something, or something hit us.' The ship went fully under and they were enveloped by the silence around them. The silence of the sea.

15. Dingy Fever

The emptiness engulfed them. The dark night was a dreamy blue, a star carpet stretching across the sky. The cool air was a relief after spending so much time indoors. The sky was on another level. It made sense why they were kept inside, having this sight taken from them. It would be hard not to dream with a view like this. To be in wonder. These feelings were new. Well, they felt new, they'd been hidden for so long inside Celine's heart.

Celine. That was her name. She'd gotten used to being called Cess on the ship. Cess-pool, that's what it reminded her of. She had a name and being there, on the dinghy, she felt more at home in the name and in her heart.

'It's interesting,' she thought. 'How having my environment controlled and hope taken away from me is shaping me.' In the moment she was *in* it. It was so real and all her senses told her that experience was real. But she was always Celine. She'd had her heart all along and the night sky had been there, looking down on her, all along. When she looked back on it, it was all so clear. And she realised this was real. She put a hand out in the dark and touched Daone on the shoulder, shocking her awake as if she had been in her own world. Had she been sleeping? She jolted and gripped the side of the boat. Ready for action.

'What, what is it? Where...?'

'It's okay,' Celine cut her off. 'I just wanted to say thank you. I'm sorry if I startled you.'

'Oh.' Daone's reply felt small. As if she wasn't expecting that kindness, or knew how to deal with it. Celine could see her shrink back into herself. Guard up. Holding onto whatever reply or thought she'd had.

'What?' Celine asked, cocking her head as if seeing her from a different angle would shed some insight into the inner workings of this woman who had beaten her and saved her life all in the same week.

'You're welcome,' Daone shoved out and turned away again, using the night and her position in the boat to drive the protective wedge back between them. Celine thought before turning away herself, *'Isn't it weird, she is this unapproachable wall and yet sometimes she seems human.'* She saw glimpses come through, where she could feel her heart.

'Why was she asking me questions?' Daone thought to herself angrily. *Wasn't it enough that I went out of my way to get her off the death ship?* Fury welled up inside her, but she held it in. The effort caused her face to strain, so she turned away, she was short and cut Celine off.

'That is the best way to deal with this. I'm so tired,' she said to herself. *'I don't want to deal with her. Maybe I could just push her overboard now. Let her bob along in the cold for a bit. That would quieten her up. Why do I have to deal with this at all? I'd better get used to it actually.*

I'm not in charge anymore. We are in uncharted territory. Before, on the ship I was in power. I had a role and I performed that role. It required me to be hard and harsh. It required me to push down any feelings of wonder and questioning. I had to have the answers and I had to have control. Now, now we are at the mercy of the ocean and like it or not I have to trust this... woman, who I see no more value in other than balancing the weight of the boat. Uh, here again, back to mean Daone.'

BANG! A sharp wave caught their small boat, shuddering the women and making their teeth chatter hard, jolting them into the now. A moment suspended in the air, still, both of them freezing to assess it and what action they needed to take to stay alive for the next moment. The boat continued its slow momentum up and down in the swell, making them both wonder where the odd wave came from. Unconsciously, they moved closer together, for the safety it brought. To not be alone and to have someone close to lean on, having both been alone for so long, even on a crowded ship for months and years.

The sea kept them for ten days. Holding them, rocking them, pushing them to their limits with exposure. The bitter cold at night and the scorching sun during the day. The storm had well and truly passed and with no sail and only oars to steer themselves, they were left to float at the mercy of the ocean. It was after that tenth night, Daone, almost possessed, sat watch at the front of the boat. Stiff as an ornament, she took a second look ahead of her. Was it a boat she saw? Bobbing in the far waves? On closer inspection it appeared as an island, far off and they were the ones bobbing, her tired brain playing tricks on her. She went to move, to turn to tell the woman, Celine, when she felt something hard hit the back of her head and the world went dark.

'*That's it,*' thought Celine. '*Take that,*' shooting hate through her eyes at the woman she loathed. She had been staring at her back for days now. She didn't know how many. She couldn't tell the time of the stars as well as Daone, she couldn't steer or have any choices on where they were headed. She had been left, almost forgotten back here, except when it was time to eat, then she knew exactly how useless she was to this woman. She was sure she regretted bringing her along. Just a waste of supplies, she could see it in her eyes, her body language whenever she took the time to turn and have that small interaction with her. That's that. She was not going back to the way things were on the ship. She was not going to be second best to everyone and 'survive' at the bottom of the food chain. Celine was already sick of it on the ship and the days spent with only her thoughts simmering and spitting had sent her into a heightened space of fever. She took the paddle and hit Daone as hard as she could as soon as an escape was in sight. The island loomed on the horizon. The still body of Daone lay crumpled in the bottom of the small boat. Now, they were going to do things her way.

16. Landing

The boat slowly lapped towards the island. The current was dragging it into the shore. Luckily the edge it was heading for was a soft sandy beach. Daone looked angrily around at Celine, craning her neck to do so as she was bound up with a rope from the boat. She was leaning on her side, facing half away from her captor at the front of the boat. The anger on her face radiated off her. How could she be doing this to her? She thought furiously to herself. After all she did for her, coming back and saving her. What was her problem? She would have asked this but her mouth was stuffed with a rag and the most she could offer was stifled complaints that were ignored by her angry, in control, slightly malnourished and dehydrated captain.

'Now, now,' Celine scolded her. 'Not long now and we will be at our new home,' she offered in a lecturing tone. 'I *will* let you go, but we just need to get a few things straight before that happens. I am *not* a slave. I will *not* be treated as *below* you any longer. I want an *equal* say and part in this little adventure we are on. We stand a better chance of surviving together, as I'm sure you know.' She paused to let this revelatory information sink in.

'Let's get used to working together and we just might make it through.' She paused, waiting for a reply (or a gesture from Daone now as she couldn't very well speak). Daone nodded. What else could she do? She felt for this woman. Could see where she was coming from and what she was going for with this action. She just wanted it to be another way. She couldn't very well trust her after this stunt she had pulled. How could she know she wouldn't slit her throat while she slept? How could she trust her to share equally what they found on the island while trying to survive? She couldn't, not right now, but she nodded anyway, deciding to deal with that later after she was untied and had her mobility back. She hated being tied up. Lack of control was not something she liked. She strove to be in as much control as possible. That's why she rose through the ranks on the ship, she had striven for more. She'd chosen to do some horrible things but they gave her more control over her daily life. Even if they made her look more out of control to others. They floated on in silence, coming ever closer to the beach and to Daone's freedom.

17. Agreements

S tillness surrounded them both. The inky black of the ocean rippled in the background. All eyes were on the beach. All four eyes. It was tense. Daone watched Celine with the blade. Walking up and down the beach. Not sure if she was deciding to untie her or kill her. She had been mumbling for hours while the boat floated into the beach.

'She was lucky,' Daone thought. There would be islands they could have sailed to that the current would have taken them straight past or the white soft beach they were now occupying would be replaced with sheer rock and pounding seas.

'If we keep being directed by this lunatic... well our luck will only get us so far,' she thought miserably, still slighted at having been tied up for so long. Celine turned for what seemed like the hundredth time and started to walk back towards her. Only this time the blade she was carrying came down behind Daone's hands and easily sliced the rope

there clean through. Daone pulled her hands in front of herself, trying to move slowly but happy she had some movement and control back.

'Well then, what now?' she asked. Celine looked at her, puzzled.

'Well you're free of course. What do *you* mean?'

'I mean, what do you have planned now? I'm supposed to just trust you and what? We go on as if nothing has happened?' Daone questioned further. 'What did you expect to happen?'

Celine tensed up, ready for a fight.

'We spoke on the boat.' she said aggressively, 'I told you this was going to be different, no more hierarchy, no more beatings. You agreed.'

'Yes I remember that. Fine. That's fine.' She shot back. 'I mean how are we supposed to trust one another? How are we supposed to have any form of balance, if the moment you feel scared or it's not going your way you tie me up and give me little choice but to agree with you?'

'You mean, if I *make* you. I'd be just as bad as you were on the ship. I lived like that for years. I slaved under your feet, as less than human, less than you, for years and you come at me like this the moment the cards are turned. The moment the shoe is on the other foot. I knew I shouldn't have let you go, let myself believe you could be any different than what you were on the ship, a monster.'

Daone took a moment of silence after this. She looked down as if letting it soak in, processing what had been said and not reacting to it.

'Yes, you are right about the ship.' She looked up into Celine's eyes and all she saw was hurt. Like she was just noticing for the first time what she had been doing for years on the ship. As if coming out of a spell.

Daone broke down. Deep sobs echoed up her throat, out into the night. Her chest heaved. Her whole body ached. Tears welled in her eyes but no tears touched her face. The sorrow didn't reach that part of her. It was deeper. Held in for many years, the way it came out it vibrated like a volcano. All around you you could feel it erupting, building in tension and movement. Until, it sounded like Daone couldn't catch her breath. Attempts to take in air became her only thought as she fought against her own despair. The darkness was coming in, taking her and she was gone.

18. WAKING

The sand blew into her face, not harshly, carried by a breeze sweeping gently over the beach. She had a thin layer of sand sitting lightly on her skin, creating a mini shell that she felt crackle when she moved. Daone sat up gently, her hands and feet free, making this process easier. Her head had been resting on a sheet of canvas that she recognised from the small boat they had arrived on. A fire of beach wood crackled nearby making the scene warm and calm. She felt fresh. As if she had been carrying around weight this whole time and now she had put it down. She still felt tired in the way one might after a long journey, but the rest had done her good. She wondered how long she had been out for, as the sky was still dark and inky as she remembered. She also wondered where Celine was. What she was. The scene felt calm and yes, she had unbound her, but there was still this tension in the air. The last years had not simply melted away and she knew there were some tough conversations to have or this history would hang in the air. She hadn't thought like this for a long time. She was so used to suppressing her emotions on the ship to survive. Any avenue of action that had an air of emotional intelligence felt foreign and the harder route to take. For so long on the ship she'd sat back and seen how it operated under the control of cruel men who thought of others as fleas, worker bees and slaves to their desires. For a long time Daone had learnt how to survive in this world by turning off her feelings, turning off her morals and operating as a tool for them. The cruel way she was, she'd adopted to survive and only now, away from that world and challenged by someone, something different, she was beginning to feel it all fall away. She was begging to sense her old self coming back and even though it felt hard and scary she wanted to take the actions that led her down that path. Slight rustling from the trees pulled Daone from her pensive thoughts and she turned to see Celine walk into the firelight.

19. WATCHING

Daone could feel herself being watched. The sun was starting to peek over the horizon. She didn't need to open her eyes for that. The heat from the sun touched her face as her body warmed from the cool night slumber. But she could tell she was being watched. Many nights and years of being around people in close quarters taught her to trust her instincts. She could feel another presence at the camp they had made. It had grown since the first days, when it was more of a collection of their items than a thought out and executed plan. Celine slept closer to the fire, with her back against the rock. Safe, when you have spent your whole life watching your own back. Daone slept in the hollow of a tree; a great monster whose base had been worn away over the years. Two great roots rose out of the ground and left a hollow that fit a body snug and tight. The tree had served her well on many occasions so far. It shielded her from the rain more than the rock as its roots swept high and the alcove set deep. All Celine had was a small overhang that kept some of the rain from dropping directly down, but not much else. So while she was protected from the back, exposure to the elements was more of a threat. She approached Celine with the idea of solving both of their shelter issues and suggested they string the tarp they had from the boat between the rock and tree. This would create a better situation for Celine and marginally improve Daone's. Daone still preferred to trade exposure to the elements for safety, being able to see a potential attack, while Celine would have danger coming from the sides, if it came.

Small things like this around the camp were strangely easy to agree on, she just had to ask. It seemed Celine was ready to work together. This confused Daone because of Celine's outbreak and subsequent arrival to the island. She couldn't shake the feeling of mistrust. She'd saved Celine, who had then knocked her out and tied her up. When was the next attack coming? One of the reasons she liked having the tree to her back and facing Celine: she could keen an eye on her. The solid mountain of rock was her constant safety. The fear, the danger was always in front, ready to be met, ready to be attacked.

20. Protecting

Neither of them wanted to be there. That was clear. They each sat across the fire from each other and pretended they weren't looking at each other. Celine felt so alone. On the ship she was surrounded by so many people and here she was constantly aware of the huge gap, the emptiness that surrounded them. Daone was not a very talkative woman and she kept mostly to herself. She had only spoken to her to propose stretching a piece of canvas from one outcrop of the cliff to above her tree, effectively creating a shelter that kept them both dry. One day the silence got to her and she half spoke, half shouted across the fire.

'What now? What are we going to do? Never talk to each other? This is silly, this is stupid!' Daone slowly put down her bowl she was eating out of and stared at Celine.

'What do you want?' She said, flat and toneless. 'I'm here aren't I? We work together. I haven't harmed you or mistreated you like you were afraid of?'

'Yes but neither have you done anything more. This isn't how people are supposed to live.' Celine replied.

'You were aboard a slave ship. What do you know about how people are supposed to live?'

'I can feel it. I just know. Don't you look at your day and feel there should be more? More than just safety and food? We haven't spoken, not properly. How are you coping? How have you not gone crazy here? We stick to our camp. We have fresh water and food nearby and have not had a *need* to explore outside of that. Is this what it's going to be like now? Is this how we grow old and die in the quiet of the night? Would you even notice in the morning, or would you just go about your day and leave me to rot under this tree?'

'She is and isn't making sense,' thought Daone. *'She can't have it both ways. She wants to be safe but she also wants adventure and to explore the island, I bet.'*

'We have survived so far keeping to ourselves. What's on this island hasn't found us and so doesn't know about us. If you want to keep living like this and staying alive this is how we do it. It would be bringing it upon ourselves to venture out and seek anything more. As for us talking, what do you want from me? You made it clear how you think of me? What value could you possibly have for a cruel creature like me? What could you get out of me besides the stories of the horrible things I've done that just make you see the deeper dark within me? I'll keep my stories to myself and you can keep your judgement.' Celine was caught between withdrawing and freezing.

'But just know you are as honourable as me. You think that just because you were a lower level than me that you should hold less guilt for what we did? We are the same and you can be as helpless and righteous as you like but power and choice come from within and you choose where to align yours.'

With that, Daone calmly turned to the side, leaned against the tree root and closed her eyes, effectively ending the conversation for Celine. She didn't have anything to say back now. Anything felt small compared to what Daone had just said. The lump in her throat wouldn't let much air in for her to even breathe, let alone reply. She sat back against her rock and stared into the fire, the white burning itself into her so that even when she closed her eyes later on, the bright flame stared out at her from behind her eyelids.

21. Windtalking

It started one night... the sounds. Small clicking sounds, small murmurs. So quiet she could easily have slept through it. She could have missed it, had she not been stirred by the increase in the wind shuffling through the trees. Small sounds hanging on the murmur of the breeze.

'Had they been here before?' Celine thought to herself. An image of small island creatures with coconut shell masks formed in her mind's eye. She could imagine all these creatures coming to get her, just waiting in the trees. Watching, when she couldn't see. Talking, and she didn't know about what. All she could do was listen and imagine all the dangers and what-ifs that lay just beyond her vision. Sometimes she would go to sleep and dream about them, only to wake and hear a rustle and know they were out there.

'We have to do something about these creatures,' Celine approached Daone one morning. Her eyes were red around the edges.

Sleep had not been present here as much as was normal. Daone didn't keep that much of a tab on Celine, but even she knew she looked tired.

'Don't know what you mean,' replied Daone, looking away. She was not going to give in and agree upon whatever was out there with this woman, no matter what she thought privately.

'Don't tell me you don't hear them too,' said Celine. 'I know that's why you've been stacking more firewood around your tree. It makes you feel safe, a bigger wall, a bigger buffer between you and the outside world. And where have your early morning rises gone? You're cinching the sleep you can in the morning, when the sun is creeping over the trees and the water. Dark enough to sleep but safe enough with the light and morning sun.'

'ALRIGHT!' Daone snapped. 'Fine. Have it your way. Yes I have heard them. No, I am not going charging off into the trees to find them. We shouldn't stray outside of this safety and explore.'

'Yes, but now they've found us, it's only a matter of time before they attack us and take us for all we have. Our camp, our bodies, we could even become slaves... again.' Celine made her case but felt the conversation slipping away from her, and her power to make any changes blew away quietly on the wind.

22. Capture

They came for her in the night. It was quiet, the trees holding their breath, the sky clouded in darkness that seeped down into the carpet of the forest, smothering sound. Quietly, they came. Out of the trees, holding the power of life and death in their hands. There was no way to stop them. There was no point in fighting. The struggle would have worn Daone out and she needed her strength for later, to escape. They must want them for something other than dying or that would have been her fate already. Hold on and survive, that was her job now. Long wooden hands. Clicking sounds like wood tapping together. The sound of their departure into the forest. She was gagged and blindfolded. Pieces of tree vines, dried and threaded, bound hands and feet. She was carried off into the night like a fog rolling into the valley and out again. She was gone.

23. Missing

Celine awoke like it was any other morning. A slight breeze pushed sand across her face. Opening her eyes, she was slightly surprised not to hear cooking sounds around the fire. Sounds of animals chirping into the day, yes. Sounds of the trees swirling wind between themselves, yes. Sounds of Daone existing, no. Odd for her not to be here, she thought. Then as the day wore on and the absence of another human presence grew larger, Celine started to realise—to know—that she wasn't alone here... and yet she was. There were others who called this island home and they had taken her companion. It was too loose of a bond to call it friendship. She felt a cold chill roll up her spine. Yes, up. This was as odd a situation as any and now shivers ran in the opposite direction too. The world was a very different place and now the game had changed. She felt a fire rise inside of her. Now, she was tired. She was sick of sitting here around her fire and waiting for life to happen to her, caught in a battle against the only other person she could see. A woman stuck in her own reality of hell. Caught in her own fight for her life.

Celine realised in that moment that there was another person here who she had not been watching out for. Had not been wary of and built defences up against and kept herself up at night thinking of ways to subdue her. This person was herself. How blindsided had she been, to have not taken more self-responsibility than now. *She* was the one who chose to go on that boat. *She* was the one who spoke back knowing full well what would happen. Poked the bear. *She* created these environments in reaction to what was happening to her. Because *she* wanted this sick outcome. On some level she knew the outcome and took the steps to get there. Now, she knew what she wanted. She wanted to be free. Wanted to act free. No matter the outcome. Instead of this scared little girl, cowering through life with her fear based actions. Tying up another woman to ask for her rights, to beg for her freedom. No, she was already free and it was within her power to reach into the day and place her foot upon the path to express that. She packed up her tools; basic weapons and food, and set off into the forest to find Daone.

24. Defeat

Daone knew she'd gone unconscious. She knew because she couldn't remember part of the trip; the most important part to her plan. She remembered the part around her camp, when she was just getting taken away. But after that, when they had started entering the unknown for her, the part that was further than what she had experienced, the furthest from her new home... she couldn't remember.

'This is terrible,' she thought. That she had given up so willingly and hadn't fought. She thought it was for the best and that she would be able to escape later if they didn't think her a threat. If she knew the way home, she would have an advantage and she would use it. But that was not the case at all now. She was alone. She had left the closest thing to a friend sleeping silently at the camp. Celine wouldn't even know where to find her. Wouldn't know where to start looking. So she wept. She hung from between two logs, tied up with a blistering headache, and she wept.

It all came down around her. The last few weeks, years of being the person she had been. Living her life and in her body, she had ruined things. She'd kept everyone out, she knew that, and she'd put up a wall and fought with anyone trying to get in. That is what had happened with the 'girl' from the ship, when she'd looked the wrong way at her and was beaten for it. It was weird. It seemed like an event happening in third person and she was watching from above, outside of herself and separated from her pain. But that pain was back now, in all its gory depths. She swung back and forth in her captives' clutches, watching them take the steps that would ultimately lead to her death.

25. Searching

I t was evident to Celine that what had come for Daone was long gone. Leaving a trail through the forest that slowly edged away from any rhyme or reason as to the path they had taken. It looked like they had come from all angles, with trees all around having broken twigs and rough bark scraped to the trunk, leaving a telltale sign that there had been a major disturbance here.

She missed her friend. There was no getting around it now. She knew she had been wrong, the way she had been treating the woman from the boat. She knew there was a different person under the facade that beat her, that was predominantly 'show' on the boat. There had been a chance taken to save each other and it was up to both of them how they showed up and contributed to that end. Celine was sure she could have done better. Could have shown up more powerfully to prevent the gap that had appeared when they'd had an opportunity to be more themselves than had been expressed in their lifetimes. From babe to adult, there was a slow crust that had formed on their skin to keep the shell, to keep the hurt and pain of the world from touching their hearts. In that moment she knew the truth and the lies of her time: That the crust keeps the truth in as well as the hurt out. That the world can be without all of a person, not some. She had been hiding on that ship and in the time left, she was going to show up and live with the courage of her heart on her sleeve and expressed as the stories on the wind.

She corralled her will and her nerves, out in the forest. She wasn't sure which was the correct path, but in her mind's eye she saw herself finding her friend and being willing to take risks to show up as herself. *This will be*, she chose.

26. Alert

The crickets sung, the distant fire crackled. A slight breeze stroked the tips of the trees. Daone felt the soft velvet of the wind roll over her as she slumped against her restraints, bound to a tree trunk. At least she was the right way up now. The rope dug into her wrists and belly as she fought against her constraints. She fought silently and subtly. She didn't want to draw more attention to herself. And she didn't want to go down without a fight. She dug her heels in and put the pressure of her body against the rope. It was no good though, it just dug tighter around her. She lost heart with each failed attempt. She knew that this was futile and that she would die here if there was not a miracle. If they could only make a mistake. If a new option didn't present itself, Daone knew she would not get out of this alive.

She could hear them singing around their fires. Even that was not a help to her, as they had travelled so far that not even the strongest wind could carry their location back to the camp, where Celine would no doubt be. Where Celine would be hiding and cowering. Why had they not taken her?

'A waste of their time probably,' she thought sourly. The drums around the fire had picked up their enthusiasm. Dread grew in Daone as she knew the time for escape was drawing to a close.

It was quiet. All Daone could hear was the buzzing of some insects around her ear. The leaf canopy shuffled steadily in the breeze. Her hair ruffled her face. She sat still, not wanting to disturb the night and not wanting to disturb the creatures that held her captive. They had sung and danced late into the night. Round and round the fire their steps and songs had taken them, the jungle shrinking away from the bold presence of their celebration. Now, the jungle crept back in. The darkness and the cold. The fear was rising as she sat, bound and at the mercy of the night. She knew she would be defenceless against an attack from an animal, big or small. She could sway her knees from side to side and shoo away bugs that came near but she could not turn back many and this weighed on her mind. Was it worth staying awake and alert this whole time if she could do nothing when the time came to act? Or was it just wasting energy for her to stay alert and follow the sound of the jungle? An unavoidable waste, she concluded, as she could not just switch off and rest. She could not give up. And that's what she saw as giving up, if she just went to sleep. Back and forth her head moved, always alert. She spent the better part of the night in this motion until she couldn't keep up anymore and she fell still and asleep, just as dawn was breaking through the trees and the sound of the birds sung her away.

27. Discovering

Celine, on the other hand, *was* moving. She was moving well and with purpose. Moving through the forest in a methodical circle, from her camp. She didn't know where the monsters had taken Daone, but she was adamant she'd find them and her friend. The camp was her starting point to move out from. Round and round she trudged. The ever widening circle made her question if she was even further from her goal or the breakthrough was just around the corner. Round and round. Well, it wasn't really a feeling of round anymore. She was going anti-clockwise so it was slightly to the left, slightly to the left, over and over now.

She came to a disturbance in the trail. Although, it didn't look like a disturbance. It was the forest organised a little too well. A little too perfectly. A stone placed back in its hole. How could she know this? But she did. There was a mark next to it where you could see it had been moved. You could see it had been pushed slightly off to the side and the sand and earth underneath showed a shallow ditch carved by this movement. A long moment passed as Celine paused, looking at this as she concluded that what she was seeing was what she was seeing. What was obvious was that she had found her first clue as to which way her adventure was unfolding. She placed a tree branch next to the stone, marking the start of her trail and the fallback position, should she need to regain her bearings as she looked for the next stage in her path. Also if it took her too far from camp, she would need markers to know how to get back. She set her centre marker and started her circles again.

Round and round, until it was slightly left, slightly left. She didn't have to wait as long as she did for her second clue. The further away, the less careful the path taken had become. A leaf broken and placed back in its place. A leaf with a mark where it shouldn't be. Animals didn't put leaves back together. They broke twigs and sticks and were resigned to leave a trace of their paths. No, the only ones smart enough to cover their tracks like this would be on purpose. And so Celine set off on her new path through the forest, each clue coming sooner than the last. Odd marker after odd marker.

28. Thinking

Daone shuddered awake in the cool morning dew of the inner island. It was colder here than on the coast, where she had spent her time acclimatising. She was dazed but she looked around and could see small human-like creatures, spread around performing various tasks. Creating a great fire. Preparing berries and paint. The berries were being turned into paint; a deep purple and a deep red. Being spread over the bodies and faces of the creators and being stored in crude wooden bowls for later. She was scared.

It had been long enough that she knew they weren't going to let her go and the sense of foreboding grew in her chest. She knew there would have to be a miracle for her to get out of this alive.

'Are they cannibals or just looking to sacrifice me?' Daone wondered. Which would she rather? Her flesh eaten and sustained a tribe of people, or to be bled like a lamb and her body offered to whatever god or gods this tribe worshipped? Such a choice. Her hands were already numb and her skin was bruised from the bonds rubbing and digging

into it. It wouldn't take much on her part to pull and break the skin, something she was not looking forward to if the moment called for it. The sun shone through the trees, the rays warming her face with its touch. Daone set about preparing herself for the day, for all was not lost. She still had her heart and mind to get herself out of this. There was still hope from the other side of the island.

29. Snailing

On the other side of the island Celine was having a time of it. The trail she was following was not an easy ride. Swamps as deep as her armpits swallowed her, sticking and pulling at her body and spirit. Was this the way they had gone? It seemed frustrating to think that she on her own was struggling, but a force could sweep into her camp and make off with a whole person and navigate this land more easily and more gracefully than her. They could be days away and with the time she was making now it would take her a week to get anywhere.

30. Deciding

I t was now; the breeze carried the noise to her. The voices of a thousand little people ready for war. Daone wondered what had changed. There had been no such signal but she could feel the change in the weather. The change in the feeling in her gut. She wondered what could possibly have changed in the sky to signal such rage inside of the island. Rocks started to fall from the outcrop above and the ocean could be heard kilometres away, smashing into rocks and sand. The island was angry and it was going to be heard. The mountain above them split at the top. Smoke started rising out of it and billowing into the air. It became thick to the touch with black tar and her nostrils started to hurt with every breath. She instantly lost her sense of smell as all she could feel was the burning of her eyes and nose. The trees started to shake with fury at being woken and disturbed from their ancient sleep. Birds took to the sky in the hundreds and moved out into the horizon, which wasn't far as the sky kept filling with the deep dark stench and mist of the fiery mountain.

It wouldn't be long now, Daone could tell. She just knew that there was fear and anger rising all around her and she needed to be away from here or she would not leave. The sound of death was tapping at her heart and making it beat more sharply with every boom of cloud escaping the confines of the earth. She decided now was the time for her. Shedding all ideas of how she could not get out, shedding all her fears of what if; she needed to make a run for it. With the strength she didn't think she had, she stood, with a flexibility she was sure was outside of her and belonged to another, she slipped her arms in front of herself. Right, now she needed to get mobile. She started hitting her ropes on the nearest sharp rock, desperate to break the bond that held her here, tethered to a death that was coming on ever so quickly. She stepped out to take her first steps to freedom.

31. Erupting

There was flame and ash raining down from above. Small pieces would land on her arm and singe and tingle. The smell of burning flesh floated on the wind. Celine looked around, her head was throbbing. Did someone hit her? Did she fall on her own and hit her head? It came back to her when she went to take a step that she had stubbed her toe and gone over by herself. Barely able to get her arms out in front of her, she'd smashed her head as she went down.

She took in the sight before her: Small creatures moved around beneath her, criss-crossing the valley in a search for something, or someone. It wasn't as if they were scared and running, they were scared and looking. It made no sense to Celine. Why wouldn't they run? Get out of the way and seek shelter on one of the mountains further away from the near-exploding one?

Celine caught a different type of movement. A small figure was dodging in and out of the bushes. Daone! Her heart leapt with the excitement of finding what she had been looking for. She watched as

Daone would read the movement of the small creatures. They almost looked like children, rushing around and leaping from one spot of cover to the next. Then Celine saw her run as the mountain rumbled, shaking the earth beneath them all and Daone caught her foot on a stone she was trying to climb. Down and over she went, smashing hard into the rock of safety she was attempting to hide behind. As the captors made their wild movement across their camp they spotted the dazed Daone lying awkwardly on her side. The shouts went up and could be heard from the cliff where Celine crouched. Woos and wahs of joy, urgency and speed reached up and put fear into her heart, replacing the excitement she'd initially felt. What were they going to do with her that was so important now, in this moment, when danger threatened from such a bigger source?

Down on the ground, the feeling of fear and confusion was shared by Daone. What was going on? Why were these small fierce people still chasing her? Why were they capturing her and binding her feet now, at this time? Why weren't they running for safety? Her heart pounded in her chest as she struggled to free her freshly bound feet and rough, raw hands from their constraints.

32. Burning

The rock and ash filled Daone's nostrils. It grated against her throat as she struggled to breath. The weight of a slab of rock was pressing firmly against her chest. She could hear the soft falling of rock, soot and the spray of something. Her eyes were covered and she shook her face gently to dislodge the residue. She opened her eyes and looked out at what had once been a solid formation of rock. A solid environment with plants and animals and insects moving about their day, unhindered by any real threat to their ecosystem. In balance and thriving. Then, this. Now, it looked like a wasteland. The sky was blackened by sooty clouds, blocking out the sun. The dark air it threw over the horizon gave an otherworld experience, like somehow they had been transported to the depths of hell and woken up without remembering the journey.

Daone tried to sit up and after heaving with what felt like more energy than she had, she took a hazy stock of her body. Bruises were already starting to come up where she had knocked and rolled over boulders. Her muscles flexed against them and gave her twangs of hurt for her trying.

The grit and coal hurt her throat. Celine jumped down off a rock to explore the scene before her. She had been better off than Daone in the recent explosion. Being further away, she was not as affected by the turbulence that occurred when the mountain spat its top into the air and started churning out chokes of smoke, barrels of coal like rocks and hot ash into the air. She cleared her lungs and the effort sent fire down her throat. The burn of the air caused her to inhale shallowly and her head spun from lack of oxygen. The screams around her kept her wholly present, her feet firmly stepping over the rocks underfoot.

The screams were coupled with the creatures skimming and scurrying around her. They were not prepared, it seemed, for this end of the world scenario that was unfolding before them. While Celine had called this island home for a few short months, this place seemed like it held more permanence for them. Generations of birth ran forward in front of Celine. They were noticeably different creatures, but you could see a resemblance between them. Family groups stuck together and made their way away from the angry mountain. No one paid her any attention besides to nudge past her as she wound her way towards where she had seen Daone. Further and further she entered the ad hoc village set against the slope. She passed more and more evidence of lifetimes and generations passed here on this rock. The vegetation proved her theory right as well as the trees that had far reaching roots that snaked their way up and down, between crevices and cracks, holding the mountain up like glue. The smell of burning wood touched her nostrils and made her think the mountain wouldn't hold up for long if the wood was burning. Images of tendrils of fire breaking and shaking the mountain filled her head and she quick-stepped her search route through.

On the opposite slope, Daone was having a very different experience of the people. It seemed to her that the traditional inhabitants were not very happy with their sacred sacrifice. A group had gathered around her and were closing in until they formed a tight knit circle that looked on with angry soot-soaked eyes. She was still tied up and although she had made some progress to improve her situation she was still relatively immobile and dragging herself through the dirt had only improved it marginally. Even with such a dire situation closing in Danoe felt fiercely alive and willing to fight to save herself.

33. WET

Celine felt the light rain starting to trickle down from the clouds. The soot was still falling and so it became dirty mud, spitting from the sky. Puddles started to form in the rock crevice on the ground. The grit and dirt ran down her face into her eyes. She dug the grit out only for more to fall in from her hair and the sky. The process repeated several more times until she finally saw through the darkness that came, when she'd lost the sight she'd relied on her whole life. Relief flooded her body as she caught sight of Daone.

The relief for Celine was short-lived. It started as a small rumbling in the ground, and it grew. The ground and rock ledges started spilling pebbles and debris down the mountain, misplacing anything not weighing more than a fist. It made walking harder as she had to get her footing firmly and it slowed her navigation to sliding. Also, it was hard dodging anything coming her way down the mountain. Her shins got hit enough times that she knew her legs would be bruised like an apple and berry crumble.

Daone struggled. Her bonds were still digging into her wrists and although she could see an exit from her current reality in the form of Celine, there was still much work to be done here. Luckily, it seemed her captors had not seen her 'friend's' approach and were arguing between themselves about what they should do. Or, that's what Daone thought, as their talk was foreign to her. They had loosened the circle around her so a few seemingly senior members could gather and converse in heated grunts and wild arm flailing. She knew this was the best time to move. Surprise would be on her side.

The hot ash had fallen thick and the grass and vine tethers were fraying at her wrist and ankles. With what felt like a stupid idea, she gathered her legs underneath herself and stood up. The effect was instantaneous. All eyes fell on her and a lopsided circle formed around her. This was fine for Daone, as Celine could sneak closer now. There was little chance of straying eyes finding her, as it seemed she was moving haphazardly, not towards her. As she stood, almost immediately the mountain rumbled extra hard and the tremors rocked Daone back and forth, toppling her sideways smashing her into the hard rock, punching the wind out of her. The small creatures looked on with a mixture of annoyance and amusement. That she had the drive left to even contemplate a future that was not dictated by them! That she could even imagine being free! Celine chose this moment. She had been working her way steadily over to the small crowd of creatures and Daone. She had seen Daone stand up and the last part of her journey was made easier, as she was not spotted in the open ground between the group and her. She stood up tall and kicked out hard. She managed to hit two of the occupiers in the head before they turned and copped on to what had happened. They swarmed back away from her, shocked. The ones further away moved in to attack, having orientated more quickly. This took the circle into a more of a wonky line. Daone fell over, a little easily, like she had allowed herself to. Celine saw why when she started rolling towards her; tripping a few captors in the process, causing more disruption in the group. They grabbed out and tried to stop their sacrifice from getting away. They eventually did dig their heels in and their grimy hands got a hold of Daone, grinding her to a halt on the slope. The pull of the mountain was against them and they struggled with the shifting floor.

The creatures struck back. They were angry and vocal and they loudly, energetically expressed this. Sharp little claws scraped Celine's legs. The clothes left over from the time on the ship and the months ground into the earth with work dissolved under the attack. The material shredded and left her legs exposed and vulnerable to more attack. Their small claws were dirty and jagged. The force of numbers was too great to hang around for long. Celine took the first few blows and stepped away, noting the fear on Daone's face as she thought she had lost her only escape. She picked up a fallen log and started swinging wildly, matching the energy of the animals she saw in front and in the way of her. She'd had enough of this situation. Her legs hurt and she was afraid of what the mountain would do if they stayed where they were. Four of the creatures fell under her splurge of craziness and force. Knocking their heads like balls, they fell on the stone, their heads cracking like melons and vile, sticky blood leaking onto the earth.

It was in this brief moment of space, when the creatures paused to see and take in the violence being dealt out to them, that Celine saw the strangest thing. Daone had bitten the closest creature's arm and taken a bite out of it. Her mouth streamed with blood and the creature howled with pain, not having expected this malicious outbreak. For all the time Daone had been docile. All they'd received had been looks that didn't hurt as much as this.

Daone was acting frantically but inside she felt guided by her actions. What she had been doing wasn't working and it was now time to try something else. This plan had just come to her and instead of talking herself out of it she just went with the energy of the moment and put some 'crazy' back on her captors.

34. Fleeing

The rock gave a gurgle of energy and shifted under their feet. Two of the creatures fell and Daone seized her chance. She slipped a knife out of the nearest's sheath, releasing them from her teeth grip as she nudged them with her hips. With the knife in hand she squatted and slit her feet apart. The vine rope struggled momentarily against the sharpened piece of slate. With her feet free, she didn't waste time focusing on her hands and skipped across the earth to the other side of the group. Celine turned at the movement and they both hightailed it out of there. They skipped and wobbled along the path, with very angry inhabitants following them. Their world was crumbling and being focussed on the retrieval of these two traitors to their vision was the control they were striving to keep. Exasperated, Daone and Celine looked back at the pack. It was frustrating that in the face of so much destruction and danger, the worst would be coming from such an annoying and blatantly pointless source; small, semi-intelligent creatures who were hellbent on capture.

35. Dodging

An almighty crack sounded from the mountain, larger than any that came before it. Celine and Daone knew what was happening. They had heard boats creak and shake, the crack of thunder that sounded like the world was breaking... and now it was. The ground under them started to split and a crevice began to form from the crack. It grew and grew, slicing the earth before and beneath them. They were due some luck and the ground started to provide it. At least now they were running together and even though the world was ending, the end result of finding each other and reuniting had been completed. There just happened to be a couple of environmental factors bearing down on them that took away some of the accomplishment of the moment. It cut short the joy of following through, and turned them to the fear of survival. A common place both of them knew, this didn't make it any less uncomfortable.

A boulder dislodged from above them and made its way down, cracking off at deep edges against the outcroppings. A jagged cannonball of pain. It just missed the two of them but a quick glance over their shoulders caught the sight of it crashing into two creatures, mercilessly taking them down the slope in a bloody mess.

'*What now?*' Celine thought. '*Quick, we need a way out of this,*' was the reply she thought quickly to herself. She sighted a river running through the centre of the camp and just knew that was the way out of this mess, for now. She signalled to Daone that the river was the new target and could see her wanting to argue with her as a cross frown occupied her face. She held onto the pain and need for control for a moment before releasing the look and nodding her agreement on the plan. She did stop and cost them precious seconds, handing her the knife and getting Celine to cut her hands so that when they reached the river, the remaining creatures were right on their tails.

'Alright alright, what now?' she said to Daone.

'You brought us here, what now?' She got shot back. Celine took a moment to take stock of her surroundings. The river cut through the camp, dog-legging suddenly at the end and curving around the base before continuing into the forest. Following it would have been silly; she felt as if the creatures would be able to cut them off through the village, even with the shaking and ash making their lives harder. It didn't matter what she thought though, as she couldn't shake the feeling that what was drawing her in and what was obvious were the hollow logs that piled on the banks around them. Grabbing one, she launched herself into the fast flowing current and held on. Daone looked on open mouthed as she sailed down the river, drawn by the current, the log holding her above the surface of the water.

'*Crazy, crazy woman,*' Daone thought, until a spear lodged into the sand a metre from her, waking her up. It was more of a warning shot to stay where she was as the creatures, it seemed, still wanted Daone alive. She didn't know what for, as it seemed a little late in the game to make a sacrifice to the mountain when it was clearly coming apart around them. She didn't want to wait to find out and grabbed a log and also threw herself into the river.

36. Freezing

Celine was struggling to keep her head above water. It was cold and it filled her mouth as she rolled with the log. It was a struggle to keep a grip on the log and she wondered if this was the right idea. At certain points her feet dragged against the sharp rocks lining the surface of the riverbed, scraping and brushing the soles and tops of her feet as she bounced along.

'*This was a painful choice that's for sure,*' she thought, hoping Daone made it in because at least she would be not alone in her fate. She whizzed down, passing the camp. The movements of the mountain felt less intense here.

Daone was in a cold, cold world. She was taxed from the nights and days she had been held against her will. She had not had any food and she gladly swallowed some water from the river. She did have an easier time with the log, as she felt natural riding on top of it and knew she would not be hit with any projectiles from the camp side— small victories in a shitty situation. She was free and would rather be in the thick of this adventure, on the run, than chained and destined to the will of the creatures who had vastly different ideas of a 'life well spent' than she did. She felt buoyed by the feeling of control she had regained by breaking free and struggling right now. It was her fight to win or lose and she felt she was on the right path, even if it was looking a little rocky. The camp life reminded her of her time on the ship. Going along with another plan that took her life from her and put her on the path of another's beck and whim.

37. Fear

Daone wasn't sure, but it seemed like she was gaining on Celine. Mayhap because Celine was dragging so much in the water. Funny how much of a hard time she was having at this when it had been her idea. Up and down her head crashed through waves and she saw the water impede her and then free her. She definitely was gaining on Celine and kept one eye on her and one eye on the natives. They were hightailing it through the village. Daone remembered being brought in and the vine bridge crossing the river she was hauled across. She knew she would have to duck dive to make it past without getting hooked on the bridge. It was a small drop into the cold water and she was terrified of going in as her feet and hands felt weighted and tired, she knew she would sink if the swaying vegetation bridge spilled them into the abyss. She hoped Celine had a plan other than riding the river to safety, as she saw several flaws. The cold water would eat away what little energy she had left and the creatures would be in a position to snag them as they passed through... that's if Celine managed to stop swallowing water long enough to make it there. She set her grip on the soggy log and gritted her teeth. She was holding on and seeing where this wild ride took her.

Celine was in pain. Her knee had jarred against a deep rock and bounced her around so now she was heading backwards. She felt the fear grow as she lost control of her sight and images of natives spearing her with rocks from behind filled her head. She almost thought letting go of the flotation log would have been a good idea because then she wouldn't stand out as much in the water. She would be more susceptible to sinking, but would it be safer? Crazy as it sounded to her, she was tempted to accept the crazy as 'safe'. She knew the fear was taking hold and clung with all her might to the log. She did see after a while that Daone was gaining on her through the waves. It took her a moment to focus on what she was seeing as she was so concentrated on herself and her situation. Daone yelled in her face and Celine had no idea what she was saying. All she did was stare back blankly and then look around to see if she could work out what was going on. The need to see behind her was strong and even when Daone reached over, grabbed her log to pull them together she still stared back, wondering how she had gotten here and how she was managing to lean on top of hers as she did. A strong fist came towards her and smashed into her face, snapping her neck back and out of her frozen fear trance.

38. Actioning

Water splashed on Celine's face, waking her to the sun in her eyes.

'What the hell happened?' She'd been racing down the river and then she was here, on this pristine white beach. The mountain could be heard in the background and the ash cloud was moving across the sky, away from her and away from the mountain. Fire spat from its mouth and changed to dust and ash before her eyes, and sailed away. A constant movement and cycle, powerful and dangerous but the process of cyclisation made it feel almost normal in front of her. She shook sand from her eyes and hair. Looking further around her she saw Daone sitting alone under a tree. A cloth bandage wrapped her arm and she was struggling to attach another strip of her pants to a cut on her hand. Celine struggled up off the sand and tottled over to the log where she was sitting.

'What happened?' She asked. Daone looked up and through gritted teeth said,

'Look, I'll tell you but can you try and not get mad? I don't have the energy to fight with you this time. I need to rest and finish what I am doing. We will have to move soon. Those creatures won't leave us alone for good.'

'Yeah, yeah,' Celine said as she looked around again. Her eyes took in the river flowing softly to touch the beach where they stood. A sand bar separated them from the ocean. The curve of the beach led away from them towards the setting sun and she wondered how big this island was and how far they had come from the hostile's camp, and even their own camp. So many questions existed and floated through her head. She felt almost light as she just stood in wonder of them all and waited for Daone to tell her what went down to get them here.

'I knocked you out, and pushed you under the water when we reached the bridge. We duck dived the logs out of reach and then when we resurfaced on the other side, I held you out and under besides your head, so they wouldn't be able to fire at you with anything.

'I think they're not very happy with you and I am still the marked one for their stupid ritual they want to do. I don't know why though, even if it did anything it seems late now.' She said this last part as she looked back over her shoulder and up the slope at the fire-breathing mountain. Its slow puff could be heard softly through the air and the slight vibrations rumbled around them, if they stood softly and felt for it. Celine was still blown away by the situation and how quickly she felt it had dissipated. She didn't press when Daone took a long break before speaking again.

'Then we rode the current all the way until it started meandering slowly. I floated you on the logs and picked up another stick to start polling us down. I tried to vary which tributaries I took when they arose as I wanted to put as much space between us and the pursuers, but be unpredictable. We reached the beach about an hour ago and I've been trying to get myself in shape to move again before you woke up.' The last part made Celine think Daone was prepared for a fight and could understand how the 'rescue' could have looked to her.

'I know why you hit me. I was panicking and would not have let you help me in that situation. I'm not mad or want a fight about it, I'm annoyed at myself. It was my idea to jump in there and I panicked. I barely held onto that log before you got there and I don't know what I would have done. I knew I didn't want to be captured, I just couldn't think. I was frozen.' She looked down at her feet and squeezed her hands together. Daone got up and put her hand on Celine's shoulder.

'It's okay,' she said. 'You did great, if you hadn't jumped in I would still be standing on that beach or be some sacrifice in the inferno right now. We both helped and we both got us here.'

39. Realising

The night crept over the beach as the two women headed off for the next day of their destinies. They walked a rough two metres apart and kept one eye on the beach ahead of them and one eye on the forest, running along the shore and behind them into the dark. Their ears were straining in the dark, aware of the slightest wrong sound or the absence of sound at all that might tell of their predators' approach and attack. They felt more prepared than they had been before. Before, they'd been compliant. Crashing through and making themselves known before knowing where they were. They'd known they were in danger, but had focussed that fear on each other rather than the true culprit. They had enemies, but so far the most dangerous had been within and the way they had acted and even existed in the world. A deep anger welled inside Celine. She knew better. She could see the way she was acting but was so caught up in being strong and fighting, she fought her only friend here. That was not what she wanted at all.

For Daone, she was at a loss. She almost felt like giving up on herself when she looked at how she had acted. She had the need to control all situations down to the minute. She needed to control and when the time came to trust the person who had most deserved it and with whom she could feel a strong bond of friendship, she had not taken that step. The leap had been left uncovered and she had betrayed that bond; first on the ship and secondly on the beach and camp. There was no need for her to act the way she did towards Celine and treat her as a threat. She could see she was hurting and understood the reason she fought for control. By tying her up, Celine strove to break that control and take back some of it for herself. She could understand and not condone. Daone saw that the way forward and to mend the possibility of what they had was not with fear and separation. Not with control and spite. The only way either of them would live through this and make a life for themselves, here or otherwise, was to act in the light of who they wanted to be. Daone wanted to be connected to her higher path. She wanted to stand at the helm of her life and be guided by her magic and not the pit of her emotional trauma.

The sun set and night descended as the pair trudged up the beach, reflecting on the life they had been watching themselves lead and the yearning to be who they truly dreamt of. Lightening cracked overhead. A hot summer storm was rolling in. It even felt like a changing of the seasons. Daone thought it was weird that she would think that at all, as she wasn't from this part of the world and she thought it odd that she should have such feelings. But these feelings had been becoming stronger. She was tapped into something else. She was connected in ways she remembered vaguely, but no solid memory came to mind.

40. Sheltering

The two women kept walking through the storm, neither wanting to be the one to call a stop to their journey. Even though they had been through a lot together and were starting to trust and change the dynamic of their relationship, there was still a rivalry. There was now too the presence of the urge to not let the other down. To not let themselves down. The waves crashed against the beach on their right and the trees blew their excess debris out onto the sand. One such huge gust thrust a giant tree to fall into their path, blocking them and either causing them to go into the ocean or forest to continue. At this point they looked at each other and shrugged. They were going to call it and stay here for the remainder of the night and storm. If they were struggling with their movement, so too would their followers. They headed into the jungle.

The ocean sprayed at their backs as they headed into the foliage. Thick trunks rose around them, blocking out the main rain yet the trickle of water still reached down to them. They were wet, tired and hungry and knew they needed to stick to the beach for now to keep any sort of bearing.

'We need to find shelter that protects us from the storm,' Daone said. Celine nodded, spanning out to her left while not straying far from Daone. There was no sense in losing each other now, after all the effort they'd gone to to find the other.

'What are we looking for?'

'Everything is wet and I don't think we're the only wildlife around. I don't know, but I'll know when I see it,' Daone replied, dropping under a rather large leaf that was drooping under the weight of the water bearing down on it. Tipping the branch, holding it to the tree as she stepped up close to the trunk, it bent and the leaf dropped all the water it was holding on the ground, diverting the water away from the centre of the tree. It was actually quite dry close to the trunk as the foliage fell away. It created a sort of cavern at the centre with a thick collection of branches and leaves protecting it from invasion of the weather. It wouldn't take much to turn this into a doable place for the night.

'Celine, this is it,' Daone called over to her.

Celine's neck snapped around at the call, prepared for trouble afoot. She calmed down as she saw Daone through the trees. It was difficult as the branches were so thick it had blocked out the vision. If she wasn't looking, she knew she would have missed her. Good for their purposes. She walked over and slipped between, into the inner part of the tree. It felt good to be working as a team. She didn't know how long it would have taken for her to find a suitable place to rest. She was not as adept at this type of survival as Daone. She was more of a 'build-it-the-way-she-was-told' when it came to shelter, not working with the environment.

She was good at finding things to eat and began by climbing the tree. It was a thick trunk with branches sprouting out in line with the floor. It wasn't long before she had bounded up the tree to see the vantage point from the top. The valley they had been swept out of on the log stretched away from her. She could see the rise on the far side of the vegetation slope up and away from them, so she knew she would be climbing later in the day tomorrow and her legs would be screaming at her to stop. She was definitely going to rest well now, if that was the case. She took note of a few other markers to help keep her bearings on the ground and set off to slither down the tree.

41. Collaborating

The thunder cracked overhead as Daone walked through the bushes surrounding their camp. She had been gathering firewood, dry sticks and larger pieces laying around close to the tree where they were hunkering down. The rain had not touched all the earth. The thick trees had stopped some of the downpour. The clouds parted briefly and she was out, taking advantage of the dry air. She looked around and tried to locate Celine. The crafty girl had been out looking for food. It was a skill of hers and Daone was keen to let her pull her weight and contribute. She was even more keen for some food and, from her time as a leader on the ship, knew it was best to give jobs to those best equipped for them. It was not that Daone couldn't find food, it was just that Celine was better at this and Daone was better at building a fire. The clouds would hide the smoke and keep them safe from their attackers. She was getting sick of running but knew that until something shifted in their favour, they would be on the back foot in this scenario and on the run. They were outnumbered, they didn't know the lay of the land beyond what they could see and they had no supplies above what they gathered in the small moments of reprieve when the environment was no good to run in. This could be a long fight and she wanted to keep moving while she was so unsure of her surroundings.

She sat down under the thick branches and took to getting the wood lit. The monotonous movements repeated over and over in this pursuit took her into a kind of meditation. It suddenly hit her as she was there: What were they going to do? How long could they run for and even then, where were they even running to? It felt exhausting even thinking about it. The endless run to nowhere. It grew like a fire in her heart as she stood there. This couldn't be the way, there had to be another option for them that ended better than running themselves out of land and into the sea. There was a possibility that over the next hill there would be nowhere left to run. She almost felt like laughing. The wild in her grew and she became giddy with her new idea. It was crazy but different and that's why she liked it. It was bold and crazy and that's why it might actually work. It was at this moment that Celine walked back into the shelter of the tree and Daone shared her wild plan.

'You want to do WHAT?' Celine yelled at her. To be honest, Daone knew this was a wild plan, but even then this response was strong.

'Are you actually crazy?' Celine went on. 'I thought it was me who would be the weak link. What am I even hearing?'

Daone just nodded and kept waiting for another response from the unsettled women. It was a bold idea and Daone was sticking to it. It was the only way she could see herself actually getting what she wanted; a resolution to this mess, not to keep running from it.

'So, what you're saying is that you want to head back the way we have come, in the middle of a storm, past the many pursuers we have and go back to their native infested camp at the end of a live mountain?'

'Yes that's exactly it,' she stated. 'We don't know how long we are going to be running from them. They know this island better than us and I want to do something other than run. At least this way we can be on the front foot. They won't be looking for us to come back into the camp. It actually feels like the right idea.'

'Well then, I bet you think I'll be coming with you? That you can just make me and I'll follow you into this mad idea? Well I won't. I've had it with you bossing me around. I can stay here and run if I want.'

'I'm not making you do anything. You are your own person and can run if you wish. This is just an idea. What will you do if you do run? What is it we are doing now? We were terrified at the camp and ran to save ourselves. I thank you, it was you who saved me and without you I would probably be dead, sizzling on the slopes of the fire mountain. But I have my freedom now, just like you and this is what I want to do with it.'

'Fine.' Celine sat down at the now roaring fire Daone had continued to grow as they were talking. The silence stretched out as Daone sat calmly in her decision to take the power and fight back to the natives. Celine sat shaking at the predicament she was in. She couldn't go back, it felt like walking into death. And to go on alone felt the same too. She knew she wouldn't sleep as she considered her two death options.

42. Rallying

The leaves rustled overhead as they hiked through the forest. Celine couldn't believe they were doing this. It felt so wrong and her body told her how against this she really was. It was an effort to force herself to walk each step. It was her mind screaming, 'No' and somehow she was being drawn deeper and deeper into this crazy plan. Daone was leading them parallel to the beach, staying hidden in the brush but oriented with the path they were taking. When they reached the river mouth her plan was to cross and head back up the river on the other side. Away from the direction they had been taking.

'But what about when we run into some very angry and hostile midgets?' Celine had argued, wary of this plan every step of the way. It all seemed crazy and even when she looked at each part in turn, they all were crazy and added up to crazy. What else was she to do? Staying where she was, death. Heading off on her own, death. She knew she would be the least favourite person for the creatures to find as she'd ruined their plan to sacrifice Daone and save the mountain.

The mountain; also an area of death they were heading back into. It was still spitting the dark smoke and fog out of its ruptured belly. She didn't even know how long they had before it started to rumble and leak fire. Moving away from the ground, shaking and dislodging rocks, Celine sensed was the sane thing to do.

'What had even turned Daone to this crazy task?' she thought. *'She was never one to risk herself for anything or anyone.'* She just couldn't get her head wrapped around this plan being for the best, couldn't see it being anything more than an unwanted risk.

43. Following

The sky cleared during the night. Daone glanced up from her feet and a star crossed the sky in front of them. It brought a contemplation, only for a moment, that was delivered to her. Why was she here? What purpose did this life have? She was nothing and something at the same time. She had done wrong. Wrong by others but more importantly, wrong by herself. She knew the standard of life and living. She felt it inherently inside her. She connected to it when she was strong and stood for what she believed in. She felt disconnected from it when she acted poorly. But it was always there; a beacon to tell her how far off track or aligned she was with her mission. That's what it felt like, a mission she was called to. The disconnect she felt in herself when she went off track didn't diminish the pull. It highlighted the distance she had put between her true life and herself. She wondered about this as she trudged along. She didn't know why she was here but she felt even more connected to the right path than she ever had. It didn't make any sense to her but she felt like she was living when she was so close to death.

The darkness felt like it was enveloping them. They sat in the forest, waiting for their time. The sun had set a while ago, its rays stretching back and touching the edges of the clouds as it left. A last claw on the day and a last effort by the day to touch the night. But night doesn't start until day ends so they never really meet and they never really touch. Like lovers lost forever from each other, running always and it never happens. The cold had crept in too and they sat on mossy earth. It took their lower extremities, then their bodies started to feel the freeze. It was at their shoulders that Daone decided it was time enough and rose slowly, shaking off the slow freeze that had settled on them as they sat waiting.

'You know the plan,' she said to Celine. A question and statement at the same time, to prompt her and double check as well as remind herself that she did, and it comforted her.

'We will only get one chance at this,' she kept going, with the obvious comments of the moment. Celine still looked passively back at her and nodded slightly. There was not much else she could do. She knew the plan. It was a wild one and she was pretty sure they were going to die. But she was committed now and she was going to do her part. They slunk out of the damp hiding spot they had chosen and trudged away into the full night.

44. Returning

The island was still rumbling as they got closer to the main peak, the vibrations increasing under their feet. The path they were on curved around to the left and small footprints were freshly made, indicating it was time they headed off the path and started picking their way through the thicker bush. The damp earth from the storm made the going easier, muffling the sound of their steps. Celine's heartbeat was sitting higher than normal and she couldn't shake the feeling this was a terrible idea and that they were going to die, with a death-bringing creature popping out at any moment from behind a tree stump or patch of leaves. The breeze cut through them and they suppressed shivers, not wanting any unnecessary movement to give them away. The sound of the camp drew them closer. High pitched chattering, small smoking fires and the stillness of the undergrowth all told them they were getting ever closer to the danger they had tried to outrun. Daone stopped up the front and moved slowly through a thick patch of foliage, motioning Celine to do the same. They peered carefully at the inhabitants of the clearing beyond.

A drizzle of rain started to patter down on the leaves through the canopy and touched them both gently on the face. The time was now. They had been hiding in the brush just outside of the camp and with the weather creating a dampening of the senses for them, they moved through the camp's edges to the other side. What sounded loud in their own ears was dulled by the rain, making them blend in with the noises of the forest. It was still a scary situation to be in, with the threat of discovery all around them. And they knew the threat of discovery was very real and that the creatures would be furious after their escape. They would not let them escape again. They might even choose to kill them rather than have them go free. Celine didn't really see it as a wonderful freedom anyway. Being chased all over the island wasn't the nicest feeling.

The mountain revealed itself to them as they climbed. The higher they went the more the village noises died down.

'Maybe the upper plato was just for ceremony,' Daone thought. The forest cleared more and the exposed rock became more and more common on the path. When they reached the river that they had escaped down, the upper village came into view... deserted.

45. Stealthing

Cicadas clicked around the camp. Tension hung in the air. Small whines of animals pierced the slow waving vegetation. The mother mountain hummed, small tremors reminding them that the worst was not over and that she was still there, powerful and vengeful for the people who had settled on the side of it. She hummed her song to sing them off into the world. Away from her. To leave the silence of renewal and the world to grow over her once more.

The two women crouched in the bushes taking this all in. They had been soaked and were almost dry again in the heat of the morning. They had been held up with the lower camp being more full than they had expected. Their new time was precious and the longer they waited, the more chance the hunting party would find their fresh trail. They might return to the camp before setting out after the women in a different direction. Both of these would result in more bodies and eyes to scout before making it to the other side of the camp and onto their destination of the mountain; the source of the sacrifices and reason for the pursuit of the two women across the island. They had been having a hard enough time just surviving on the island, being hunted was the straw that meant this camel could no longer walk. They had to devise a way to negate this threat to their lives.

46. WINDING

It was crazy to Celine that they were doing this, creeping back into the lair of the enemy when they had spent so much energy getting out. She had been knocked unconscious, ridden down a freezing river and braved the death of spears, then run for days through the jungle. All of this and Daone was still not happy with her. What would it take? Now they were back in the thick of the danger zone and the tension between them was high. She was trying to subdue herself and put her thoughts and feelings aside for the good of the mission, the shared goal. But this time it wasn't working. She remembered the time on the boat when she was punished by Daone for speaking out, even just looking at Daone would have gotten her a beating and shoved below deck. The pain of the memory grew fires behind her eyes and she stumbled on a rock she should have seen in the momentary lapse of self-awareness. It earned her a sharp glance back from Daone and had it not scared her just as much she would have said something very loud and very detrimental to the balance of the partnership at the present time. This situation felt very much out of her control and at the same time there was this irking feeling that this was not where she was meant to be. There was a better way to be handling this and it was her way. This was Daone's way and what suited her. In a way, this wasn't even Celine's fight. The creatures had focused on Daone and probably wouldn't even chase Celine if she left now. Why did she feel a distorted sense of loyalty to this woman who, besides a few well-timed actions that benefited the both of them, seemed to have nothing but utter contempt or not a care in the world for her? The thought wouldn't move anymore for now and she sat with the feeling as she wound her way, more carefully, higher into the rocky mountain landscape.

47. Reminding

The wind swept over the mountain, bringing a coolness to the ground that permeated up into Celine's bones. She had spent the better part of the day reflecting on her options. She finally felt she had found peace within herself and knew what she was going to do, for now at least. She walked over to Daone who was crouching nearby, waiting for the right time to go on. Resting, until the last push up the mountain could be made. She made no attempt to be quiet as she made her way over and Daone looked at her angrily as she approached. It was weird, because Celine couldn't understand why she looked angry until she realised why they were there, and what they had been working towards the whole day and last couple of days.

'Just remind me what we are doing here?' Celine asked.

'What do you mean?' Daone asked incredulously. 'I told you before. We spoke about it yesterday and I explained it all.'

'Yes, yes, can you just go over it again for me? I just want to be clear for myself.'

'*They,*' Daone motioned to the village, 'obviously want me for this little ritual they were going to perform here. I want to know why, so if there is a chance we can alter their ways of thinking, then we can get out of here alive and they can stop chasing us.'

'Ohh okay, yeah I remember. And what's the plan for me? What do you want me to do?' Celine followed on.

'Okay, okay. So I obviously can't go wandering around too much, as I am the one they want. So you are going to go into the crater and poke around. See what you can make out and if there is anything you can bring back for me to examine. Anything that tells us what is going on. Do you understand your role?'

'Yes and what happens if I get seen or find I have company in there?'

'Well, you want to be careful, obviously, as I can't do much from here. Like I said, if they find me I'm in more danger than you, so we have to be careful. If you can, make the, "*Hey hey*" sound real loud so I can get away from here as quickly as possible. And make sure you don't make your way back here and be followed. Obviously for the reasons I mentioned.'

'Right, yep I've got it. Okay, no worries.' Celine went to wait by herself on a rock, still sure of herself but feeling more confident because of the conversation she'd just had.

48. Tremoring

The rumbling in the mountain began again in earnest as Celine walked away from the spot she and Daone had been hiding in. It was only minor but she could feel the earth tremor, reminding her of its power, sitting just below the surface. It steeled Celine with her plan, knowing the great power of Mother Earth was cheering her on.

'I can do this,' she said to herself. She knew this was it and her moment to do something on her path that felt right, and she actually felt sure of herself. The rocks became more of a feature on the landscape and she passed less brush and trees. A noise like someone displacing a stone caught her ear over on her left. It drew her eyes to a boulder, about ten metres away. Curious, Celine stopped the direction she was walking in and started creeping up on the boulder.

'Who's there?' she whispered sharply, thinking maybe Daone was following her all along, using her as a type of bait. She wouldn't put it past her.

'Meeshee bop,' came the reply, making Celine freeze in her tracks. She waited for more but it didn't come, so she asked again, a little less sure of herself now.

'Who goes there?'

'Meesheego bop' was the reply she heard. Things were getting weird and off plan. She had no idea who this was and if it wasn't Daone chances were they were not going to be friendly. Even if it was Daone, there was no guarantee of it being friendly. Celine was frustrated at being challenged so early into her new plan and sense of control over her future. She put her common sense aside and strode up to the rock and peered around the other side of it. What she saw made her step back and start, for there was one of the tiny creatures—what looked to her a child—looking up at her. She had perched on an instep cut into the rock and appeared to be waiting for someone to pass this spot. Celine could tell that this was a small girl child, as her features were quite dainty and her huge eyes that she had yet to grow into were held in wonder at Celine. Things were just getting weirder and that's when she heard the other voices. Not here but over behind her, in the direction she had come from. Louder male voices getting closer over the hill.

49. Disconnecting

Sitting in the bushes just off the road, up the hill, Daone was getting worried. She had been able to hear voices for a while now and even though she did have the plan of following Celine from a distance and using her to flush out what was in front of them, she was at a loss as to her next move. If she left now she would be at the mercy of the people on the trail. If there was a long stretch of no cover she would be caught out in the open, and hunted. She was paralysed with fear. Her hand kept twitching as if she should move and then her fear took over and she jerked back into her original position. The voices got louder and Daone didn't even raise her head as they passed by. She felt swallowed by the terror that gripped her, turning her into a small child who hid under the blankets when afraid. She was much the same, hiding as low and as disconnected as possible in the rough bush.

Celine was astonished. This little creature was blowing what she knew about the vicious creatures out of the water. She calmly looked at Celine, knowing the voices were coming closer but not bothered by her standing there. She stepped down off the rock and motioned for Celine to follow her, her little arms and hands waving, inviting Celine to conceal herself behind the rock. There was a path that led away from them, the boulder having concealed its existence. It was a less used track with branches overhanging, but this added to its secrecy as no one would be able to notice it from the main path she had come from.

The rain started as they were walking up the path. A light drizzle that sat on top of the clothes they were wearing, but not heavy enough to soak through. It caught on the wind and the crags and rocks, swirling it around them, a hazy mini storm. Celine knew that this would get worse when the rain increased, as they were quite exposed and the storm would prevent them hearing if anyone was around them. She was pretty confident she was okay for now, as the path they had taken had led them away from the one she had been on and the sound of a hunting group making their way up the path had died away the further they got on their route. She kept following this smaller childlike creature. She had a wandering way of walking where she moved from side to side on the path and was in no particular hurry now.

Celine made a noise with her throat like clearing it and the child turned her large eyes to her as she walked in her strange floating fashion, finding her way with her feet gripping and keeping to the track without looking. Celine motioned at the path, to see where they were going. The girl just shrugged back as if she didn't know where they were going or didn't know what Celine was saying. Celine wasn't sure and thought she just didn't want to tell her out here. It did prickle at Celine. Still, she was not bothered enough to say anything and she kept trundling along.

50. Regretting

The wind blew over the mountain as Daone scurried through the bushes. She had to keep ahead of the people coming behind while also being aware of the people in front. Not wanting to be met with either, the bristles scratched her skin and deep red marks now littered her arms, she could only guess what her face and neck must look like. She was scared; she had told Celine to go on ahead and tried to use her to flush out any potential danger but now she couldn't find where she had gone. She was more afraid for herself and it was a dim care that grew for the missing Celine. It didn't make sense. Why would she not be here anymore? There was the path and she had no hope of getting anywhere without being on the path. Unless she was hiding along it in the small brush like she had been. The feeling of unease and deception grew in Daone.

'Of course that's what she has done.' It was what Daone had done; hidden and used her companion for her own ends. Why wouldn't she do the same back to her? She should have expected this. She had

gotten complacent after the time spent on shore. She should not have forgotten the same Celine who knocked her out and tied her up on the boat. When she was pushed into a corner, she acted with desperation. Of course she would hide and abandon Daone the first chance she could get.

Daone stood in the middle of the path, panting slightly and frozen. What should she do? Stay trapped in the low bush with who knows how many dangerous creatures milling around, or keep going? She chose to keep going. She was a fighter. She prepped herself to meet whoever was coming on the path, and she prepped herself to fight Celine, if she ever saw her again. She would not be getting away with this. This was the last time she would stab her in the back and get away with it. The anger welled inside of her as she stepped around the next bend. Soft dust settled into her drying wounds.

The wind was calming where Celine was on the mountain and it made hearing the voices carried on it harder and harder. Celine was getting more and more agitated as they went farther down the hidden side track. She'd taken a chance in coming and she wanted to know things. Where were they going? Who was this child and why was she helping her? With every step, the idea grew in her that she could be getting taken to some strange private party where they would eat her. They could have planned all this to get her to follow. Or they could be trying to separate the two women from each other. Daone was back there, hiding and waiting for her to come and tell her if everything was okay. It was her doubt in that plan that kept her going. Daone was using her, there was that idea too. Celine was sick of all the lies and deception and she wasn't sure who to trust or what to do. Or where this path, following Stumpy—that's what she would refer to her as in her head—was taking her.

The clouds and darkness started to come in at once. The wind was picking up and Celine felt a shiver move down her spine as she followed Stumpy. The pace had slowed and as Stumpy came up to a rock face, she suddenly stepped into the rock and disappeared!

'No way,' Celine thought. She had fallen behind in her anger and gotten lost in her head. As she got closer, she was amazed to realise there was an entrance concealed in the rock. There was no way anyone would see this from afar; it was perfectly camouflaged. There was a deeper entry and more to this path than she could see. There was a flickering light and the sound of a flint scratching repeatedly on rock. The flame took and Stumpy was illuminated in the small alcove. The rest of the tunnel stretched away into the gloom but this looked like some sort of entryway where torches and supplies could be stored. You could just walk in here, out of the weather, and pick up what you needed. The wind was even less here, which was surprising as it should have formed a gusting power... but nothing. It was as if a door had been closed.

'Weird,' she thought, but Celine wasn't complaining as she was not dressed to function very well in bad weather. She also didn't enjoy it very much. She enjoyed a more comfortable time. The wind howled outside and interestingly, a warm breeze emanated from within the tunnel. She had unfrozen enough to have feeling in her body. Stumpy headed off and Celine padded after her as the soft earth of the tunnel took them deeper into the mountain. She hoped it was going to keep going like this. Feeling her fingers and toes again was a nice change

from being at the whim of the elements on this tempestuous mountain.

51. Holding

Daone was irritated. She was now laying flat to avoid detection and the group of creatures who had come around the bend had now set up a small camp where they would definitely see her if she were to step out and try and get away in either direction. They were waiting for something, that much was apparent. Only facing outwards from the circle they had made, the majority of the group were looking towards the mountain. The steep rocks in the area made it impossible to climb but still, they started into the mountain's cliffs. A couple of them watched the backs of the group; sullen youngsters too afraid of letting the elders down and too low in the pecking order to be afforded the good view. Daone settled in and while she was irritated she was equally bored and equally tired. This had been a long day, attached to a long couple of days, and she was nodding off after a few minutes of this anti-climatic show.

It was quieter in the tunnels. Celine could feel the ground shaking slightly and she could hear the growing sound of voices from deeper in the tunnel. Stumpy was growing excited the nearer she got to the voices, picking up in speed and doing a double tap of her feet as she almost skipped through the turns. A glowing light emanated from up ahead. Celine was nervous now, as the only contact she'd had with creatures and people from this island had been hostile, except for Stumpy. She even felt bad as she thought of the little one's name, as she had been kind to her so far. It was weird to have so many mixed emotions, as only just before she'd been frustrated and about to confront her guide. The longer she hung in there when things got tense, the more they seemed to pop and she moved onto another feeling or emotion coming up. It made her less connected to her emotions as they came and went, and she could just hang in there with her end goal and what she wanted. As soon as they rounded the next bend, the light grew considerably so that she would be able to see even if the torch being held was taken away. Stumpy ran off ahead, the excitement built in her until she seemed to take her bubbling self and bounce off down the tunnel. Celine stood stunned, listening to the babble and cackle of words tossed around, flinging off the walls.

As the noise of the babbling hit the cave up ahead—she assumed it was a cave as she could see the start of it appearing—the chanting stopped abruptly. The flickering of lights gave away that people, something or someone, were moving fast up ahead. She considered running away, hightailing it back along the path through the rock, but felt better of it. If she was going to continually run she was always going to end up on the run. If she wanted a different result, now might be the best time to figure out what was going on around here and what she could do to take back some power in this situation.

She'd had a fractured relationship with Daone, who she knew was using her for her own ends. She knew Daone had sent her up the path to flush out anyone ahead and make sure the path was clear for her. If Celine was clued in about what was going on here, she might be able to help her friend instead of being a tool to her fear-based actions. Plus, this little creature had not shown any harm to her and was instead sheltering her and bringing her into this secret cave system out of a rather blustery storm growing above. Celine knew she was set in her decision and hoped she was right as she broached the lip of the tunnel and stepped out into... darkness.

What?

As Daone was lying on the ground getting colder and colder, she dreamed. Her sleep was fitful and she woke many times, afraid she would give herself away in her slumber. The fear of losing time kept her on the edge of getting any real rest. She would drop her head and when she felt like she raised it a second later, the males she was watching were in different positions. It meant she was losing track of herself. She felt like she should stay awake properly but no matter how focused she thought she was, she dropped time and track of people like butter melting in her hands. It reached a crescendo and she smashed her head on a rock, unaware she had lulled so far. The next thing she realised, she was groggily opening her eyes... and started with a shock.

Two lime green pale eyes were staring back at her. The eyes of the main leader were there. It was not the warlord leader; she knew from watching them before. This was more of a shamanic leader. The medicine man. As such, he was adorned with such things as feathers, frog bones, small and arranged in diamonds around his neck. He had a snake tattoo adorning his arms and each follower had one snake curling around their left shoulder. This was startling enough for Daone, but yet it was more so by the sound he was making. A *slithsss-tut* rolled around in her ears and she could hear the footsteps of others joining their medicine king. The storm carried the rancid stench of their clothes and green paint adorning their bodies. She knew there was no point running. She had been here before, but she couldn't stop the involuntary pain and spasm of her chest as the anguish and fear of her situation enveloped her, pulling her into fierce shakes as tears sprung from her eyes. A small yelp and sob quickly followed, as she was strung up by her feet and legs and carried away up the mountain into the oncoming storm. She knew things were bad as she had never been this far before. She had only been in the village, waiting around. This scared her, seeing all the men dressed up. There were some women too scattered in, dressed and painted the same as the men. The women were strange, with stripes of black streaking past the green paint. They made an eerie addition to the clan, no less fearsome than the others. The wind swept around her raggedy clothes and bare arms, biting at her scorned flesh. The tufts of grass and footprints of her captors were the last things she remembered as a heavy woven sack was pulled tightly over her head and fastened alarmingly tightly around her neck. She then passed out, unable to stay with the pain and torment of her current reality, preferring the refuse of her unconscious mind to the unknown of reality.

52. Helping

There were drums. Celine knew that they'd started back up as she entered the room, but the lights were all extinguished. It took her eyes precious moments to adjust as it was not total darkness she found herself in, but minimal. A gloom of blue emanating from cloud shaped stones in the middle of an oval shaped room, moving away from her in each direction. She found herself in the middle surrounded by many. How many? She would guess at hundreds of slightly different ones. They were shorter than the other tribe, which was unfortunate for them as they were already so much smaller than the average person already. With that lessening in height they had also gained some width, making them seem like squat versions. Their hair was silver and grey. Even the young ones took on this eerie older appearance that made them look smarter than they gave off. They had an air of wisdom, but it was more Celine's perception as the smaller children still gave off youthful smiles and energy. This made Celine look more closely at Stumpy.

Following her, she had assumed she was a child but now, looking at her alongside the rest of her people, she was actually a normal sized woman. This got her thinking that she had actually been hoodwinked a bit, was lulled into a sense of safety by the youth presented to her. She knew she'd followed due to this false sense.

Celine motioned to the group gathered around the stones, the closest. Motioning to the room and to the stones and to everything. She just wanted to know what was going on and there was no real reference point as to what they had in common. They were strange compared to the creatures outside. She had outrun the others and been up close and personal when she had fought her way through. She had only just met these stranger creatures and was more out of her depth than she realised.

'What can we do for you?' The main chief stepped forward. She heard it and saw it at two different speeds, as her mind couldn't comprehend what she was hearing and seeing. How did they speak her language? Mouth agape and an incredulous frown forming on her face, she said nothing and just let the silence hang in the air between them. Well, mostly silence, as people were still milling around and caught up in their own conversations and observation of her.

'What do you want?' The chief with his blue painted face and feather headband asked her again. She was taking in more and more about this strange situation. It was almost as if she could only take on so much at once and she was noticing other things as she went along.

The roof of the cave was so weird. It bubbled down into the overhanging space. Like the clouds, the rocks in front of her were bulbous shaped. Even smaller bubbles formed out of the larger swaths that struck through the roof. It made it look like they were in the clouds, how real it made her feel.

'I... I don't know who you are,' she stammered to the chief. 'I know where we are, in the side of the mountain, down, but not who you are. Are you like the others out there?' She motioned back the way she had come, but not knowing exactly the direction she was actually referring to she started mentioning all around her so as to cover ever availability. Her questions had come on fast, building on each other and pouring out of her. She paused after realising she had asked for more than one thing. Composing herself she stood up tall and shifted her shoulders back. Her slouching was a sign of how uncomfortable she was and she regathered herself and stood waiting for a reply.

'We are the people of Blue Mountain,' he replied. 'We are referred to by others far from here, by the Serpent tribe; as the Swahlie-Tong. It is a word used to describe the uniqueness and openness we foster here but to them, it makes us weak and able to be controlled.'

'Wow, just wow. This is a lot of information.' Celine had not heard another's voice in so long, other than Daone's. The information was astounding when she had previously known so little about this island and its inhabitants... even that it had inhabitants!

'What else can you tell me about the island? Where are we, how do we get off? What goes on here?' Again the questions came fast and the chief only replied to the ones that frustrated her more.

'We are a people of creation. We are here in our hearts and live in our hearts. Our formation here is to be connected to each other and be connected to our upper star. Our above queen.'

'Your queen above, what does she do?'

'Sharp and to the point I see how they want to play this,' she thought.

'She is the ruler. But she does not rule how you are used to. We do not offer morsels of matter to be paraded over by others. We are a people connected to our hearts. We offer up ourselves in service to our hearts. We offer up ourselves in service to the one truth. Our truth.' He said this and motioned with his hands inside himself and out into the room, then up into the sky rocks.

'How do you do this?' she asked.

At this he shook his head and turned with his inner posse of mostly old, wrinkled friends. There were two exceptions to this description and they were two warriors. She assumed they were warriors by the leather plated armour that hung off their bodies. They were modestly dressed and one was clearly male, one clearly female, though their clothing still only revealed the same of each: hands and necks. The rest of them was either covered by clothes or armour. Blue paint edged the amour. Deep blue like night. The group shuffled out and Celine was left standing with the rest of the tribe. She was a little stunned and unsure of what to do. The group remaining started chanting and drumming again and the people milled around, chatting and pointing at the newcomer in their midst. At that point, Stumpy stepped out from wherever she had been hiding and motioned for her to follow. Celine flung her hands up in exasperation and followed her through the crowd.

53. Roasting

The world looked different from her perspective. Daone was hanging upside down over a pile of rocks. It frightened her for a moment as she thought the rocks were a fire by the way they were arranged. A quick self-assessment of her perceived burning flesh came back negative and she relaxed momentarily into the ropes holding her hands and feet on the wooden pole. Shit, she was here again. Immobile and at the mercy of the tribe's people and their crazy king. As she thought about this, she caught sight of the rancid medicine man walking through the camp. His skeletal frame stalked towards her as he noticed her looking at him. His long slender fingers reached and stroked her hair, pushing it behind her ears, freeing up her face. He leant in, his stench overpowering her. The rotting was putrid. The moment he was close enough to her so no one else could hear he whispered, 'Tik toel shmanga,' to her. It was a weird noise, as she was not used to hearing much from them besides shouts and what she imagined to be abuse. She had no idea what this recent sound was meaning but only could guess, as a shiver went down her spine, that it couldn't be good. There was no misunderstanding here, no bringing her back to camp for a purpose other than pain or a violation of her. Her body reacted to this and she spasmed and jerked away. Her head came down and hit him high in the forehead, bursting the skin and bringing blood pooling onto him. It was strange; he did not move. Did not flinch. The blood pooled and his eyes still stared straight through her, like she was a demon and only she knew she was physically there. Maybe that's what they thought of her; a demon to be vanquished while she looked at them and saw the same. Demons all around.

54. Suffocating

The cave system Celine found herself in was vast. There was a meeting of tunnels that lead off in many directions and levels as they sloped up and down as well. It was a maze and she would have found herself getting lost were it not for her guide Stumpy, who was leading the way firmly and fast. She knew exactly where she was going and even the curious people around her who sought to stop her couldn't slow her down. She still walked just as fast and luckily for her, they didn't step in her way for long, moving aside as she came through. Hands reached and grabbed at Celine's clothes and arms as she passed. Not enough to hinder or stop her, but enough to take her attention. Her energy was low and she was sick of it all after what felt like a long time. It was so big for them to still be travelling in this way and passing people; the cave must have been enormous.

Eventually they came to their exit, stepping off their route and through a smaller doorway. She thought it must have been a doorway as they entered what appeared to be a home entrance. The door led to a sitting area and small seats had been carved out of the rock, providing a circle of seats backed by the walls. Beyond the circle was a door, of sorts. The doors here were big enough that Celine could walk through and she realised how strange that was. These people didn't need tall doorways, yet they had them. It dawned in her that maybe they hadn't built their tunnels; someone else had. Or they had built them with someone taller in mind. A man was seated inside. He had the same grey hair as the rest of his people, and an air of calm wisdom about him. Stumpy placed her hand on his shoulder, leaning in to touch her forehead to his. It was an intimate movement that signified an intimate relationship and shared bond. She turned to Celine and said plainly and articulately, albeit accented in her native tongue, 'Welcome. This is where you will stay while you are here. This is Hanuk, my soul partner. I am Reekei.'

Celine was stunned. This kept happening; she kept having ideas of what was going on and they kept getting shattered. She realised she was standing there with her mouth open and shut it, gathering her thoughts.

'Oh, I thought you couldn't talk,' she ended up saying. Realising she was wasting a good first impression she then said, 'I am Celine. Why did you not speak to me before?'

'We were forbidden. We are not of the tall order. I am just a servant to them. I sought you out and brought you here. That was my job. They then tell me the next part of the plan and I obey. I am not here to fill you in on all, I am here to look after you. Keep you here until we are told the next part of the proclamation.'

'What proclamation?' Celine had the creeping sensation of being part of something far greater than she'd realised, and she wasn't sure yet how she felt about it. Things had taken so many unexpected turns.

'There is a tale of a woman. She will come here and free us. Free us of this cave system that we are subject to. We lived once above in the jungle and land. We were one with it and loved the freedom we had to stare at the stars and breathe the fresh air. Then danger came. We are here. We have fallen back to our sacred stones and monument to the truth. To the heart of hearts. This is where we have found refuge and this is where we have been.'

'How long have you been here?'

'Twenty seasons of big rains. That is when it rains for more than a moon. The land is turned to swamps and the land soaks up the water and fills the trees with life. It has not rained like this in many moons. But we remember and wait for the time when this woman comes and creates new life, new land that we can move to.'

'Wait, what do you mean new land? Where is this new land coming from?'

'We would be free if there was new land for us to go to. We cannot go above with the Serpunt-Foe fighting and killing us. We have gatherers who get what we need, but mostly we are fed by underwater springs, underwater creatures that we harvest from the caves.'

'And you live here all the time, but I saw you above ground? What were you doing there?'

'We have spies who can see out of the mountain. Parts of it are broken away rocks and we saw you coming up the mountain. I was sent out to find you. Bring you back here for the chosen masters. They are the group of people you spoke with earlier.'

'Well I wouldn't really call it much of a conversation. They told me next to nothing and left me with you. They didn't even all speak to me, just this chosen spokesperson. How am I meant to get out of here? And where am I meant to go? This island is cursed and I've had nothing but bad experiences since I got here.'

'What do you mean get out? You can't leave, we need you to free us and send the Serpunts away. We need you to help our people. We are not cave dwellers by nature. We are not meant to spend so long underground, scratching a life out of these rocks. They are magical and a place of worship to our people. Now they have become a living tomb that sees us trapped here, dying or facing worse than death outside.'

Celine listened to this rant of Reekei's. Seeing her get worked up about her people made her quieten and listen. She was wary of insulting her or disagreeing with her too much. She was still glad to be here, rather than the blistering cold storm outside, or at the mercy of a deathly tribe, or even being led by her very helpful friend who sought to put her in harm's way every chance she got. She wondered about Daone now and hoped she was at least away from the storm and waiting somewhere safe. From the sound of it nowhere was really safe here on this part of the island. She wondered how they had stayed so safe for so long where they landed. So long ago, that trip and landing felt like. She had changed so much. Her spirit was lost on that ship and now here she was, conversing with these tribal people. She nodded her head to Reekei and Hanuk.

Celine sat down and stared at the fire lamps strung around the room. This was where she was right now. She took in the room and her circumstances and felt the warmth of her surroundings calming her. She leant her head against the wall and took the bowl of fish-style soup handed to her. Still contemplating this, she absentmindedly consumed the soup and felt herself nod off gently. The toll of the last few days was giving a heavy lid to her eyes. She shut them and was gone, not feeling the soft hands catch her head and carry her away.

Celine woke with a start, snapping her eyes open and taking in her surroundings quickly. She was on high alert, forgetting where she was; a bed in an alcove, just off the main room where she had been sitting. It was a comfortable setting. Soft animal furs had been arranged and as well as the doors, this space was suited to someone of her height. A mount had been made for her head to lean on and she could feel the cosy warmth of the room reach out and envelope her. She had even been given a soft shift to replace her tattered and ratted clothes. She had no idea how long she had been there and slipped out to stand in the main room. Hanuk was still there, sitting strong and stout despite his grey hair. She noted an elder wisdom emanating from him.

'What are you doing here?' she asked. As if she needed to. It was clear he was watching, either for her to leave or for someone to come in. She wanted to strike up a conversation with this man to see if she could learn more about her situation. He was not a big speaker it seemed. He inclined his head to acknowledge her speaking but was not forthcoming with a response. She tried a different tack.

'May I have my clothes back?' she asked. Even though it was nice wearing something else, she'd felt comfortable in her clothes and wanted to be ready for any chance she had to get away. She didn't know if she would actually leave if given the chance to be away, but it was nice to have options.

'Gone,' he said. 'We get you more when you have bathed.' She frowned at him. She had known she smelt but the power of fear and exhaustion had pushed it from her list of priorities. She knelt down and gathered some furs to warm her as she sat with him.

'What can you tell me then? Anything?'

'It is not for me to tell you the workings of this place. You will see it for yourself when Reekei comes to take you. She is also resting back there.' He motioned behind him at the passage entering the rest of the abode.

'When can we go?'

'Soon. She was not as tired as you, but being away from here she worries about me and will take longer to sleep when she is troubled so.'

'Okay, we wait then.' Celine shifted to sit and listen to the hustle and bustle of feet and voices outside the cave.

Noises filtered through and she imagined a community forced underground but still existing. Things needed doing, errands run, food made and people talked away as they did so. It was obvious they were not dying left right and centre, but she could only imagine what it must be like out there. The hub and bub and what it all looked like. Even if she did get out, it would take many days and months to explore and see the wonders of these cave systems. The rest rejuvenated her and she was ready to explore. Now she just had to wait for her guide.

55. IRRITATING

There was a painful and scratching sensation on her skin. The rocks the women had woven into a top scratched her already raw skin. The scabs that had begun to form over her torn skin were tearing off and new wounds were criss-crossing her old ones. Their sticks had strands of woven rocks and they were being swung around as they sang—or rather, chanted—a sombre song of pain.

That is how it came through to Daone, who was swinging slightly in the breeze left over from the storm of the day. It had raged as she had hung there, bitter cold biting into her and the rain soaking her until she was numb. At least that was a reprieve from the pain of her blood running out of her hands and feet and pooling in other parts of her body. The vulnerability she had been feeling had faded too. She didn't have the energy to care anymore. If these people wanted to offer her up as some sort of sacrifice to stop ground tremors uprising or whatever it was, that didn't matter anymore. It would put her out of her misery. She couldn't take this anymore. At least if she stopped fighting it would be quick, she hoped. What if they kept her here for months? Tethered to stones and trunks. Leered at, played with by their medicine man. Even as she thought of it she became even smaller. Smaller and smaller until she drifted off again. The blood ran cold in her veins. Cold from the weather and cold from her dying spirit.

56. The Chosen

Celine awoke with a start. She had fallen asleep again. This time no one had made the effort to move her and she realised it must have only been for a short time. Hanuk was sitting opposite her and when she woke, he rose and walked out the door. This was timed perfectly as Reekei entered from further in the home and came up to her.

'We must go now,' she stated, face plain and neutral.

'Where are we going?'

'It is time to bathe and then meet again with the Council of Chosen Ones.' This caused a nervous twinge in Celine's heart. What did these people want with her? The question flashed through her mind again as she followed Reekei out into the hustle and bustle. It had died down as the day had worn on. She assumed it was day, as when she had come in it was early morning. It seemed people had less to do now and she could move through more easily with less people stopping and staring. Reaching out to touch her as she passed was still a thing.

She followed Reekei down a long way. They took different passages this time, constantly at a downward angle. She wondered how far they could keep going. She was about to reach forward and grab her shoulder to ask but as she thought of doing this, Reekei turned and put her hand out to touch her lightly, just above the collar on her right side.

'You must not speak past this point until we enter the pools. I will help you and show you what to do.' Confused, she was going to ask what Reekei was talking about when they stepped through a side opening door, adorned with animal bones, gems, and plain rocks, cut and polished to resemble fancy rocks. The room opened up in front of her to a huge cavernous area. It was not like the one she had been in earlier. This one was more of a natural shape and style, stretching away into the distance and even falling into darkness the further it went on. The torches in their hands and on the walls extended only so far.

Water gurgled in pools all over the cavern. Smoke rose slowly up, making it appear to Celine that she could actually see the temperature of the water. There were groups of people huddled together all over, bathing and relaxing in the pools. It looked like a great time. The air hung at a warmer temperature than the tunnels and there must have been vents that lead out into the open from this one, as the tunnels were still cool.

The idea of such an enormous life-giving mountain living here when she'd thought they were mostly alone and in an unknown place was crazy, and kind of creepy to Celine. She looked over at Reekei to see what she was doing or leading her to next. She motioned for her to get undressed and together they entered a pool, halfway between the light entrance and the darkness of the rest of the cavern. They only set up a certain number of torches as they needed, instead of lighting up the whole space. It created an invisible line of where Celine should go and should not, as she could see people were huddled in with the centre light. She wondered what could possibly be out in the dark.

The tunnels and system seemed like a gift and such a magical place to be, but if the Swahlie-Tong saw it as a slow death and something they needed to be saved from, there must have been more to it than she could see and comprehend. The water pooled up around her chest. It was higher on Reekei. She saw her keep to the side of the pool they had chosen, whereas the centre gave Celine the most depth for her tired and sore muscles to soak in. She looked around and as she made her way past the other woman's face, she saw her looking at her, watching her.

'What do you think of this place?' Reekei asked. Celine sat with this for a moment, still looking around. She was warm and comfortable, aware she would be in a relaxed state and could be manipulated to be more open than she should be. This was the first time she had been asked what she thought and not just ordered around and given limited information.

'I see it as a great room,' she said slowly. A frown creased Reekei's face and Celine knew she needed to do better.

'It feels sad,' she conceded. 'To be able to come and visit such a place would be a dream. You can feel the magic of the place and your people obviously love it here.' She motioned her hand at the people in the other bathing stations, as it was true. Compared to the tunnels and frightened faces she'd seen in the cavern from the council, these people here were happy. The tone of their voices, the touching and the auras they gave off were of apparent happiness. But she felt sad.

'Even when I was on the surface, running for my life and being told what to do, I was free. Here the people, they're stuck underground. When was the last time they went out in the open air? When was the last time they saw the stars? You were allowed out but it was dangerous for you. You had to risk yourself to find me for a purpose. You were not free.' At this, Reekei lowered her head and nodded.

'You see it also. It is sadness. We are trapped here with the Serpunt Tribe above.'

'Why don't you fight them?' Celine asked. 'You have the numbers, there are many people here and from what I have seen from above you could stand a chance?'

'It is not the numbers that matter here,' Reekei replied. 'We have more than the Snake Tribe. We are a people with weakness. We have dropped into weakness and the council harbours these thoughts and ideas.' A shiver was travelling down Celine's spine as she was told this. Even as she was still submerged in the hot water of the pool, a cold was trapped in her bones. This was not just an ordinary conversation. This was an interrogation. She could feel the fingers of revolution reach out and touch her today as it had on the boat, so long ago now. Her compliance or confrontation of the matter would affect her viability here and her safety.

'What of the council?' she asked, knowing she needed to keep her host talking before she gave an indication one way or the other. It could be a trap set by the council to test her loyalty here. Which was absurd as they had brought her here, but that's what her nerves were telling her. She was caught up in thinking and missed the start of the reply.

'... do not have cause for action. While here, they have control over the people. They are masters and the people slaves, even if they do not see it. They gave up their free will and right to many things when they came here.' The mood of the conversation had taken a downward trajectory since they had begun. It just seemed to get worse and worse. If Celine knew this was going to be what she faced here, she might not have been as accommodating to her host when she'd met her outside in the open. She was annoyed that she was being drawn into another problem when she'd initially wanted to run away from the tribe and danger. It was Daone who had chosen to turn back. She knew she'd then chosen to ignore her feelings and head into danger, but there was a bitterness that stayed.

Celine's focus made it hard to be open to anything Reekei was saying. She let out a sigh and Reekei saw this and continued speaking even more animatedly.

'This is a real problem for us. We are trapped here and you may seem free but now you have to help us.'

'What do you mean? Are you saying the same as the council? That I will be the saviour?'

'No, no, you do not understand, you are not listening to me. Forget the council for a moment. They only want to make things worse and keep everyone here. We need you to leave. We need you to be gone and *not* be this magical leader and teacher and saviour. Proving that the council is wrong and taking all power from them will save us. If you do as they say they will kill you.'

'What do you mean? I am not safe even here, doing what they want?'

'No. You are a pawn for them to keep control here. They like the control. They have had opportunities to rally and to fight and each time they have turned them down. Even the warriors selected for council do nothing. They do not fight and we have come to realise they never will. The only fight they are interested in is the one that is dirty and backstabbing and is keeping us here. A fight of control. It wouldn't surprise me if they were in league with the Snake Tribe.'

'What is going on here?' A voice came strongly and directly from above them. Celine startled and looked behind her, snapping her neck through the water. It was the female warrior from the council, fully dressed in armour and holding a long pole with a blade the length of her foot fastened to the end. It was shiny metal and looked really sharp, not something she wanted to mess with. It increased the aura of danger the warrior gave off. Reekei stood and answered for them both.

'We were talking of the lakes. The monsters in the far lakes that we must be wary of.' She gathered her clothes and stood waiting for Celine to exit the water. The silence stretched on as she moved. Celine was not sure if the question still remained unanswered and was being waited on by the warrior, or if there was more to be said.

'We do not need to speak of such things. We will take great care of you, Light of Stars.'

The name was weird and unnatural to Celine. She had not been referred to as the Light of Stars before and wondered what other people here had projected on her persona or purpose, to their own imaginations. The warrior looked down into the water where Celine had been, thinking, it seemed. When she was done she snapped her neck and looked straight at Celine.

'Very well. We are done here. Your presence is requested by the council. You will make your way to the throne room shortly after the first bell. Then we will talk and see what great things you will do. The saviour of the people—hurrah!' She ended this statement with a curt nod of the head, turned on her heels and stalked out of the room. The people around moved out of the way and conversations hushed and fell as she walked. Celine could tell it was not a normal occurrence to have this type of presence down here. She looked on in amazement and prepared to ask yet another question to Reekei, as the more information she got the more questions she had.

'What do you mean by "monsters" and what does that mean when she says, "The first bell?"'

'It means don't worry about the monsters. We have not heard or seen any in many moons and as for the bell, you will see or rather feel that one.'

'What do you mea...' She cut herself short, mid sentence and stood still. She could feel the ground moving. She could feel it under her feet and she could see the surface of the pools ripple and move out. It was as if the mountain was rumbling internally and the whole place shook and vibrated.

'This is the bell,' Reekei said. 'If you hadn't figured it out yet. It happens many times a day and at the same moment. Thus we are able to tell you to be somewhere based on which bell is going off. This one is the first one as it is the first in the day. You will get used to it. Many say the mountain is talking to us and that we can decipher other messages from it. It understands if we are good or if we are evil.' Reekei paused and let the information sink in.

'If we keep the Snake Tribe at bay we can influence its ways and make them better for the people who live here. It is a crude way of keeping track when you are so used to the stars, but the mountain takes care of us and we toil here day after day. A slave to her beautiful safety.'

What she was saying felt true and Celine knew that now she would be able to go to the council and ask more questions and get some more information. She was glad these conversations had happened with Reekei as now she would have more ammunition to go with. If she could have information that led her to be in more power with those who had power, she would be able to ask the right questions and get the right results. She wanted out of here and she needed some help to get there... even if she had to bend some corners.

The walls of the caves all looked the same. It was a wonder to Celine how Reekei could tell the difference and where to go. They had hightailed it back to their accommodation where a change of clothes was provided for her, before they were on the move again heading up and up. There might have been a pecking order based on stature in place there as the lower they went, the lower the entryways were. The quality of the clothes got better as they ascended and even what people were doing. They had makers of all sorts of things. The ingenuity of the tribe was amazing. They used all the different resources of the underground to make the different pieces for their community and life. It looked like they must have had tribespeople who took the risk to go above, as some things had to have been gotten from there. Wood for some of the tools stood out as a main one and the frames and doors along the passage were ornately crafted. They decorated the passage and light reflected off curves and crevices, giving it an eerie feel in darker spots. It made her curious as to what they burnt down here for light. What oil or such? As far as she knew, there were no whales down here. She was firm that she was going to find this out when she was back in the rooms with her guide. It might prove invaluable when planning. The caves got further and further apart as they got lower. Prime real estate bought you more room. At last, they came to a different door than the one she'd first entered from the large, oval ceremonial space. This door was dark, with knurls and faces carved all along its edges. In the middle was a red orb, the glow from the lights dancing across its curved surface.

'Where are we?' Celine asked. Again she was told what they wanted to tell her and not what she wanted to know.

'This is it. Be ready.' And at that, Reekei walked off. After all they had been through it was underwhelming to have her leave in such an easy way.

Celine pushed open the door and eyes turned to face her as she entered a small cavern, circular in shape with a huge table in the centre. The table was roundish in nature. It almost looked like a shrub, the edges generally forming a shape but still ragged and wonky on the outside. It gave the rugged look of a natural material. She looked at the eyes all staring at her and put faces to the council she'd met briefly the day before.

'What am I doing here?' She asked, loudly and firmly but not accusingly. She did not want to give away what little leverage she perceived she had from her quick and interrupted conversation with Reekei in the baths. The room had a murmur of whispers and shared glances around it. The tribe was bristly and agitated. Some looked as if they were holding back the urge to speak out to her. The warriors shifted slightly. They looked uncomfortable sitting and she noticed their weapons hanging up on a wall nearby to them. They hung on what looked like purpose-built holders. Celine surmised they must meet here regularly for the need of such a holder. The silence was broken by a male who looked similar to the one who'd spoken to her before.

'We do not want to talk about that in great detail now. The time will come and we have a request to ask of you, but until then we have other things to talk about. We have knowledge that we wish to pass on to you and we would like to know more about you, if you would permit us to ask. Why don't you have a seat and we can discuss further?'

Celine immediately got a sense of this male being untrustworthy. He did not wait for answers to implied questions, he just spoke as if she would obey. When she hesitated he got irritated and it flashed across his face before he repeated himself with an effort at calming his tone. She saw through him, but was at a loss as to what was going on and was resigned to not having the most leverage now that she was down here. She walked over and sat in the chair that was indicated for her. It was tight, even though it was the largest of the seats here, obviously made for someone bigger than all of the occupants.

'We wanted to thank you.' A female spoke from over on her left. She was dressed in a golden shawl that hung down over her seat. It gave her an opulent look and if they had been above ground she knew it would have shone in the sunlight. Down here it made her look out of place, like she was wishing she were somewhere else. Celine wondered if others noticed.

'You have come to us at a great moment in our time. The time is perfect for us to make an attempt to be out of here. To make an attempt on the Snake Tribe. I am Shewonda and I sit on this council. So it is.'

Another female stood and spoke.

'I am Triwigil, I look after the homes here. I sit on the council. As it is true that we are poorly down here, we need to make the surface safe again or we must have more resources to fulfil our people here. We are in a great time of need. The council member Shewonda was just talking of our current peril, and it is good of her to do so.' The look she threw at Shewonda was harsh, it could have been used to pitch onto the decks of a boat and wipe it clean within a short time. What was going on here was not a matter agreed upon by all.

The mountain spoke to them. It was a shaking they could feel underfoot that grew in the room. No one thought much of it until it did not subside like the last times. It extended and looks of worry spread throughout the room. No one moved and there was a tense silence where Celine could feel herself holding her breath. She relaxed herself and started breathing normally. It was some tense minutes later when the shaking stopped. The looks flashed around the room again and the female warrior stood to leave for the door. The one who had seemed in charge and who had been silent for this meeting stood, and the rest of the room froze. This was a sign of someone in charge or who held a sense of authority over this council.

'You will remain here with the group,' he said, aiming it at the warrior and, Celine could feel, at her. It was an instruction more than a command and yet the warrior sat back, albeit with agitation on her face. Celine was still not much wiser than when she'd come so she didn't want to go anywhere anyway, unless it was away from here altogether. It made her think maybe there was a way out through this room and she should remember how to get here. The door she'd come through did look special but she didn't remember seeing any locks. The council sat in silence as the lead male left the room. He was gone for a short while before returning looking troubled.

'We have many things to inform you about, but we must break for today. There are urgent matters to attend to. Sharlone here will accompany you and fill you in where it is agreed upon.'

Celine got up and left through the now open door. It was just a hint of an answer and then no more. She needed more to escape. Behind her, the female warrior stood.

'This way,' she pointed down the hallway. It led to another hallway and room opening. Round, with puffed out edges.

'You will sit.' The floor was cold. Celine looked up and waited for more. It came through gritted teeth.

'I will tell you what I am allowed to. Nothing more, so keep your questions to yourself. They are not for me. You will be here until we can find a way for you to be of use to us. Useful in the way that you help keep the people safe. They are fixated on the idea of getting out of here and it keeps us in control. We can do our jobs and keep them safe but we cannot allow them to go out into the island as they will be killed by the Snake Tribe. We do not have the same killer instinct that they have used against us. They will die if they go out there... A gruesome death. They have very many ways to kill and none of them spare the person of pain. They are part of the rituals used to keep their tribes under the spell of strength, the spell of darkness that inhabits this island. They will follow you to the farthest reaches of the island, and they will find you if your wish is to leave here.'

The woman looked down upon her and Celine felt that this last part may have been added in since she'd been with Reekei in the bathing chamber pools. She did not know how much this warrior had overheard, if anything, but it would not be wise to cross her. It was chilling for her to imagine the effects and the reach of this tribe. She did not know where she was safe or what she could do. Even underground she was not safe. She would die down here and it would not be great for her companion Daone above as if she had not been found before, she would surely be soon.

'Do you know there is another?' Celine asked. She knew she must risk it or Daone could be left all alone. If they saved her they might go back and save another. Smack. The backhand of this leather clad warrior smashed down and threw her off balance. Her face smacked the ground and throbbed. This was not how she'd imagined this conversation going for her. The violence was a shock she was not expecting and it dazed her. She slipped out of consciousness for a few moments and when she was back the conversation started up again.

'Now, when I said I had things to tell you, that meant that I would be speaking. You will be telling the people that you have been above to fight for them, to free them.' Smack. Another backhand threw her the other way. This was ridiculous. She was supposed to be helping them and she didn't understand why this was happening. The ground pooled with her blood and held her face as a pillow while she kept trying to grasp in her mind what was going on. Was this her future, to be held here and made to look like she was helping the people when really their own leaders were stringing them along? Making it seem they were being given hope when the falsities of their actions actually kept them prisoners and slaves for longer? This situation was the same as she'd found herself in, onboard the ship. A slave as part of the masses. The last kick sent her into darkness. Her thoughts muddled up. She knew there was more to this story but she couldn't put her finger on it. It slipped away from her as darkness bore in.

57. Hallucinating

It was a terrible time Daone was having. The singing seemed to go on forever and she wondered when these creatures slept, if they did at all. It was torment having them come up to her, poke and probe and rip small tracks along her skin. She was tired. Dead tired. Her bones hurt and her skin was a rippling flame crossing her body. There was a paste of the shaman mixed with green plants pulled from somewhere wet, as they stank of mold and dripped murky water. He came up to her in intervals when she was looking especially weak and rubbed this mush into her sores. The pain intensified at this point and she rolled her eyes into the back of her head.

The Medicine King walked up to one of the others standing watch at the side. He motioned to the prisoner and spoke in his native language. Two of the other tribe members nearby heard and walked over to the tied up woman. They cut her bonds and let her fall roughly to the floor. The rock was not forgiving on her body and she knocked her head. She was definitely not waking up soon. They lifted her up and strapped her to a rock, her legs tied at the bottom and her arms at the top. They gave her enough rope to fall to the floor, her body limp and weak, before walking away, leaving the original captor and Medicine King standing there. The king lit a stack of plants on fire and waved them over the unconscious Daone. He then left too and the sounds died away. The sound of the celebrating tribe could still be heard in the distance but, for the moment, the darkness of night started to fall and the restless night noises started to move in and take the day's place. The temperature began to drop and settle in with dew and damp.

58. Rising

Back in the cave, Celine was just coming around after slamming her face into the ground. She was not sure how long she had lost of her life by being knocked out but she felt the anger rising inside of herself. Another situation where she felt like she had no control. There were people who wanted something of her, they wanted to control her and so far, they were succeeding. She had no escape plan and nowhere to go if she even did escape. She wasn't sure if Daone was still alive and she had no plan for changing any of these circumstances. She wasn't even sure of the alliances of the people she had met. Was Reekei telling her the truth, or was she being manipulated by everyone? The weight of the evidence that people were against her weighed heavily on her and she wasn't sure what to do. The cave where she was lying was darker now. The torches had burnt and dimmed and no one had bothered to top them up. She raised her head and looked around, noticing a figure standing down the hallway, half keeping an eye on her and half keeping an eye on the other direction.

Seeing Celine stir, they turned and walked towards her. It was the male warrior from the council. She did not speak, only looked up at him as he walked over. She was not in the mood for another beating and needed time to gather a plan. He stood looking over her and motioned for her to rise. She did and he pointed away down the tunnel, back into the lair of the Blue tribe. Back to the weight of her responsibilities as this leader and saviour of the people. She felt like such a fake figurehead as she walked back through the people. They talked and they pointed when she passed. They looked at her skull, bruised and battered. There was blood congealing on her clothes and her eye felt like it was getting puffy. The warrior kept a strong pace behind her and even though it looked like she was the one leading and triumphantly heading through the tunnels she knew she would be in trouble if she acted in defiance of the council. The deeper she went, she noticed the conditions go from fair to worse. The houses closed in and the doors met each other more tightly until she reached the one she recognised as Hanuk and Reekei's. She entered and saw the two of them sitting on the earthen rock stools, conversing in quiet tones. They looked up when she entered and a look of disappointment spread across their faces. Reekei looked away and Hanuk spoke.

'Clean yourself through there.' He pointed to a small room off the main one. When she entered it contained a bowl carved out of the rock. In it was a pool of water and it was held in place by a wooden plug that fit perfectly in the base of the sink. She washed her face, wincing at the cool water stinging her skin where it was torn and embracing the cool as it numbered her face where it was bruised, which was in many places. When she was done she made her way back into the main area and set up on a stool.

'What now?' she asked. She also looked out into the hallway she had come from and saw the warrior standing just outside, down the way. The same way he had been standing in the hallway; one eye on the door, one eye on the hallway. Alert and giving off an air of capability. No one would want to mess with him.

'Now we wait until they need you again. This will not be it. The people will not be happy with merely trying, there will have to be some other progress made. There will need to be a story shared that inflicts knowledge on the people. In some way they need to choose for themselves that staying underground is a good idea and that will pacify them. It may not be the safest time for us all here, so watch yourself when you are out as well. This cave where you are staying is well known to the others. I would not put it past the council to organise something to happen here. They are sneaky and cunning. Keep your wits about you. Hanuk will sit up while we rest and keep an eye out. You may return to where you slept last night. The bell of the evening will be ringing soon.'

'Very well,' Celine replied shortly. She was exhausted and it was obvious she had been out of it for a while if it was evening again. She was still getting the hang of keeping time down here and she was not sure of the bells yet either. It was a subtlety she would need to be more careful of picking up.

59. Lying

It was a deceit. The ropes were not tied tightly; they only looked like they were. They could easily be slipped and taken off her wrists. Daone was dumbly staring at her wrists and past them to her feet. She was lying on her side where she had fallen and woken up. She was weak and did not want to draw attention to herself by moving. She rolled slightly and brought into her vision the two guards she had heard milling around, stepping lightly behind her. She saw them as warriors, fierce and mean. They had been some of the main ones toying with her before. Cutting her and leaving wounds for the Medicine King to come and put his poison potion into her skin. She wondered at the effects of such a magical paste. She was even wondering if maybe this was all an illusion and she was imagining being here, or even imagining the ropes being loose enough to get out off. What if she did something stupid while under the influence of some magic medicine potion rub and she was off in another land right now? She was in danger and her senses were not to be trusted. But what could she do? Stay here and be slaughtered painfully—and it appeared slowly—or stumble about and sort something else out.

There was a noise from the opposite direction of the group gathering and the two guards' heads snapped around to look in that direction, taking in the sound and eyes searching for more information on what was going on over there. It was quiet so any noise stood out. The space held sound really well and it would spread down to where they were if triggered in the right spots. The sound of rocks being disturbed loomed nearby and the guards both bolted towards it. It seemed there was more of a threat there that needed both of them than the woman in front of them. This was her chance though and Daone sat straight up and slipped the ropes off her legs and then over her hands.

'*That was easy,*' she thought. '*What next?*' She stood tenderly on her jelly legs and looked around. There weren't many places she could go. Everywhere she went they found her and she wasn't even sure where Celine was because she hadn't seen or heard from her in days. It would be reasonable that she had run off and the tribe did not care for her, only for hunting Daone. It would also be believable if they'd just killed her for helping Daone escape the first time and then she really would be alone. She heard noise coming from behind the boulder and footsteps scraping along the floor. Out from behind the boulder, where her ropes were secured, stepped the other guard whom the Medicine King was talking to earlier. Talking was a generous description, as she wasn't sure what that communication method actually was. Wave and make noise. This was a tense moment and Daone stood, her muscles tensing and relaxing, ready to make a move and take on an adversary or take off.

'Come.. wi.. th... me.' The voice was not smooth. It was broken and stop-start. It was rough and even though she was surprised to hear a voice she understood she also second guessed actually hearing it. Was this part of the magic? Was he even standing there, as tall as her shoulders and lithe and strong? Ready to fight and having honed this skill and other physical attributes through a life lived in harsh outdoor conditions, she moved to a side step to get a different perspective. Maybe she was still tied up and couldn't actually leave, maybe she was still asleep and viewing the scene from above or outside of her body. She had heard tales on the ships of such experiences. Such magic existed on islands, tall tales told on winter evenings to keep the cold at bay and the minds active.

The warrior shifted on his feet slightly so he was still facing her and repeated his command, he seemed irritated at her but the choice was hers as to her actions, it was not a command.

'Come with me.' This time Daone was sure she heard it and decided this was what she was going with. She stepped towards him and he pivoted, so she could pass without him showing her his back. So they were not friends and she had to watch him. Maybe they were going to a tribal celebration and this was all organised. She felt like that wasn't true, as she didn't know why they would not just come to her. They had been there all day, poking and prodding. What would they have left to do here? They didn't even know if she was awake. Was she awake? She looked back to where the ropes had been discarded on the stone floor and imagined seeing herself lying there, prone and constrained. She didn't feel it in her wrists and her legs transported her across the ground and out of the clearing. She stepped into the bushes and disappeared from the view of the main area. The bush got thick fast and she could hear the light footsteps of the warrior pacing behind her. She must have been going the right way as she was never corrected and she did not hear any other commands for many minutes. What she did hear was a piercing scream from behind her back at the camp. She had been discovered missing, she assumed, and tensed again to run. The hand from behind reached through the space between Daone's arm and torso and held her back. There was no violence in it, it was merely a reminder to walk and not to run frantically away. They must be going for stealth and not all out fear, like she was used to.

There was a small grouping of boulders jutting out of the ground up ahead. The plants grew thick around them and she had to push back deep foliage to get close to them. She was guided this way by the mysterious camp intruder and she kept pushing through, careful not to make noise and keeping her wits about her, as much as she could while up to her ears in magic potions. She touched rock and could go no further. She looked back at her accomplice as he was pushing her to the side and stepping along the rock. At some points along she would bend down and look at little scratches on the rock, reading, it looked like. He could use the markings to find more and at one point he passed a marking that looked like a circular shell curling into itself. He stepped out from the rock, padded the floor with his foot, and reached out to touch the branch of a tree fallen on the ground. It was especially hostile looking, with thorns sticking out of its sides every which way. He gripped the thorny handle and lifted. She thought it was odd to be collecting firewood at this time and thought maybe they were making a bonfire to burn her at the stake. Was it good luck for them to bring her along to help? But no, something even more magical happened. The whole stick lifted off the floor and took some of the ground with it, opening up a hole in the floor that stretched away into blackness. He took one step and jumped in. Just like that, the scowling man had disappeared into the ground and Daone was left standing there with nowhere to go and no one to make her go anywhere.

She looked around and contemplated running. She really was free now and she would be able to get away. She was not sure where the hunting party was, as she had not heard any crashing through the forest after her. She stood there for moments, taking in the silence of the forest and the noises of the forest. Silent from the deadly force she knew would be after her and overwhelming with the noise of the abundant life that filled this part. This was no barren rock face now. This was prime bug and animal territory. She realised she had been dreaming through a drug-induced haze for a while and nothing had happened. No one had jumped out and no one was telling her what to do. If she winged it and ran, the tribe would be after her quickly and she was in no condition to be outrunning anyone. She looked at the hole, made a quick decision in that moment and jumped in after the man, reaching her arm back up after herself to cover her tracks and close the hole behind her.

60. Showing

The boulder above shook. It was moving. It was moving because it was actually hollow and there were people above stomping their feet as they moved along it. It was a way people moved through the thick scrub as nothing grew on it. Daone was underground but it was more like a carved space within the rock. It created a cavity that sheltered the ones inside from the outside, but still allowed some noise and feedback from above. The space was lit by a torch that had its light spreading out from the centre. The angry tribesman was standing in the middle with the same displeased look on his face, but less anger. The tension in the space was less than it had been outside when she was tied up, and it could almost be felt to dissipate completely. This was a different dynamic and Daone was just figuring out what was going on as another chute popped open on the opposite side and a black-dressed figure popped their head out.

This was one with obvious traits of the Serpunt tribe but was not made up in the same garb and paint. Looking at this one and then comparing him to the angry warrior clad alongside, they looked almost normal, aside from having squashed features and stature. They motioned for a quick follow and the paint-clad warrior stood back and left space for Daone to climb past into the hole. She moved closer, eager to see where this was leading and was met with a direct descent down a wooden ladder bound with fibrous roots and woven stems. Even though the materials were of a degradable nature, they seemed sturdy to hold and Daone concluded they must have been maintained regularly, making them safe and reliable for constant use. The space was so odd and obscure, she wondered why they would want to use it so much. Again, she had the thought that this might be all in her imagination and she might wake up tied to a stake, but those thoughts were getting less regular as she went along. The magic green paste must have been wearing off, or she was becoming more lucid and okay with whatever was thrown at her.

61. Judging

The sky outside clouded over. The black painted figures, smelling of rot and death, snuck in and sucked out the fresh air. Heavy air, marking the approaching storm, sunk onto the people above ground. It was humming with energy as the greatest storm these elders had ever seen descended upon the mountain. They could feel it growing and whipping up the vegetation into a frenzy. The people below never knew and could never know the chaos that ensued above. The mountain absorbed the noise and the sound and all the people ever felt inside was the rhythmic shudder that announced the coming and the going of the day and night. The people below kept going with their lives and the people above, on the ground, battened down and braced. The world was angry with her pelting of rain. Judgement was here.

62. Descending

Daone followed her guide. She couldn't see much, as the torch light was blocked by the body holding it in front of her. She felt, rather than saw, the next rung in the ladder and she maintained a strong hold with her hands and feet when shifting her position.

'Where are we going?' she asked. Her speech was slightly slurred. She was glad it was only her facial muscles that suffered the ill effects as this shaft looked like it was quite long, and she wouldn't want to fall. Even though the guide looked solid and strong she was still a damned sight heavier than they and she did not want to test their strength. She was unsure whether they were male or female as the light had been pretty weak earlier as well. Did it really matter though? If they were aggressive and a threat to her they could be of either gender. She was not sure she could fight off anyone in her state.

'I must also look a state,' she thought as she caught a glimpse of her hands after a shard of light hit her hands. Dirt was crusted over them, concealing any trace of her skin colour. Her eyes felt crusty too, as if

the dirt was keeping her face shielded against anything, a thick layer caked on top from her escapades. Probably from lying in the dirt and having the wind whip around her too.

63. Quiet

The mountain shuddered a final time for the night and its inhabitants went to organise sleep. It was easy to fall into the rhythm of mountain life and Celine found herself going about the motions. She followed what her guide told her to do; picking up the moss-like peat that acted as their fuel source down here. The smoke was sweet and taken up chutes that were cut into the rock. It looked like water had wound its way down through the rock and dripped on the floor, creating natural air holes that took the smoke from the fires and cleansed the air. The mountain system showed itself more and more to her as she spent more time there.

The day had been long. She had taken in as much as her puffy eye had allowed her. Her guide did not have much sympathy for her and averted her eyes as much as she could with Celine around. It was like she had gone from a saviour to a burden overnight. The energy she gave off to Celine was cold and resigned. Like she knew she had to have her there but was just happy to get it over with. Get her out of here as quickly as possible. This was not someone she was open to having around and there was a wall between them now.

The night was getting on and Celine knew she was about to be ushered into her bed cave that hung off the main room. She stood up before she could be asked. They looked up at her from around the fire and focused in on her for the first time really that day, snapped out of their own little world by her forward momentum.

'I didn't ask for this,' she stated. 'I wanted to leave and find somewhere safe to escape to. I did not want to be your saviour. You found me and brought me here. The least you could do is help me leave if you don't want me here either.' She did not wait for a reply and crawled into her spot. She rolled to face away from them and the exit and settled in for the night, aware of their faces and stares burning into her back. She had made them an offer. She had staked her freedom on these people who were not her fans. But she was relying on more. That they hated the bureaucracy here and that the pain of their current reality would motivate them more than the pain of fear. They were safe here but trapped, and might risk it if they felt they could make this life better for themselves, with the possibility of freedom.

The cave remained silent. The remaining occupants staring at the back of their now fiery 'saviour,' who had been a hope and now a burden. A reminder that they were trapped and held here with all the others as slaves. If they could not be free from this, then maybe there was nothing to lose by helping this angry giant. A shared look between them and they spent the remainder of their night staring into the flames, each contemplating the reality they found themselves in and connecting with their hope for the future. Which would win out, they wondered.

64. Quest

The wind continued to grow and the growling of thunder swept across the island. Trees shed their weakest leaves and they sliced through the air, hunting all that was in their path. The waters on the coast pounded against the shores and the rivers that normally fed out into the ocean stretched themselves and had water smash and meet them at the shore. The villagers who sat along the river moved their shelters and tents further from the shore, as the river swelled from the extra water and their homes were more susceptible. They huddled together in their tents and wondered what they had done to anger the gods so.

They had lost their sacrifice, again. This woman was a blessing and a curse to them. A blessing that they would have found someone who fit the description of the saviour. And a curse that no matter they had found her so many times, they would be destined to lose her. A thought crossed some of their minds and was shared over the sound of the storm. Were they to be forever cursed to live like this? To sacrifice people and be separate from the tribe of the blue? The tribe of their brothers and sisters whom they tried to save and whom they had lost for so long, possibly forever. They disappeared many seasons ago and had not been seen since.

They prayed and they were loyal to the guidance of the Medicine King. They used his advice as lore and they worshiped the gods with all they had. What else would it take to have the tribes as whole again? There was magic of the Blue people. There would be trade and laughter and the young men would fight against each other and prepare for the transition to manhood. To serve in their tribes was the greatest honour they could have and now the tribe was weaker without them. Who would have thought that honouring the gods would turn out this way?

The sacrifices started early on. They were the early way for the gods to be pleased, as told by the great ruler. The king. He would have ceremonies and go deep into the netherworld, conversing and gaining knowledge for the tribes to bring back and help them take control of the island. The days following these early rituals were powerful. The people felt the power of the words and of the spirit drink they would be allowed to consume. Through drinking it they felt the connection to the divine and now they yearned for it. The king gave it out on special occasions and one of those was when the main woman was in their care. The divine potion would flow freely in the camp and all would be well. It felt like they could catch the night fires in the sky. One tent had a particularly rowdy set of families.

The young boy who spoke drifted around the tent, connecting with the eyes of many. He did not look away and he spoke passionately about the state of affairs in the tribe.

'He takes so much of our freedom and what does he give us in return?' he asked. 'The people have been miserable but they say nothing and follow the guidance of this old fool.' A gasp came from the side of his vision and he spun around quickly to address the old woman and young girl huddled there.

'He does nothing for us except keep us addicted to his divine potion. I have tasted this potion and seen what he sees. There is nothing divine about it except the divine way in which we all give up. We are weak and under the spell of this medicine king. A king not worthy of us as his subject. We are the divine ones. We are powerful. We have knowledge that could have us run this island how we want. With nature.'

He pauses to let the words sink in before continuing.

'She is angry at us, mother of the nature. She yells at us and shakes our mountain with this storm. Her tears fall against the roof of this tent, sadness at what we have become.'

'But what of the ancient ways?' asked the girl. She was less afraid of these outbursts than her grandmother. She stood and met him in the middle of the circle. Standing by the fire, she was illuminated and her beauty even at such a young age shone through. Her fierceness was noted as well, because no one else stood up and challenged this young leader in the camp. They had heard him speak before. At the start they thought nothing of it and as time had gone on they had feared to say anything, should people think they supported his ideas. They had been on a hard journey since the parting of the tribes, it was not lost on them that the young ones who knew little of the struggle of the past would speak up now, naive in their ways.

'We should do something different.' She stated plainly and for all to hear. She did not look away. She did not lower her voice. The lightning crackled as if in reply to her and the storm raged on while the people were swung in another direction that night.

65. Fearing

The mountain shaking worried Celine. She looked up and saw the glowing embers of the fire lightly illuminate the sitting area beyond her sleeping spot. The walls had shadows cast on them and she could see the faint outline of someone moving softly towards the opposite edge of the cave, the one that went through to the main interior and where her guide and partner slept. She wasn't sure of the rest as she had never been in further than the washroom, if you could call it that. She enjoyed the hot springs much more than the cold trickle of water that made its way down through the rock.

She rose gently, making sure to keep her feet soft on the ground. Not wanting to disturb the possible intruder. She crossed the room quickly and stood at the entrance, peering into the gloom. Her eyes adjusted to the even darker surroundings and picked out the form heading through another doorway of her 'home' complex. This doorway was shorter than the others, marking them as an area she was not welcome. A person as tall as Celine would have had to duck. She stood, listening for any sign that they had noticed her and were waiting for her to approach. She could hear nothing and so moved on. It was pointless to try and guess where they had come from. She barely knew what was outside of the cave she was in, let alone where she was going outside or where they had come from. She knew she mustn't be popular with everyone but she found it hard to imagine why anyone would be in here looking for her. She looked through yet another door and collided with the back of a very solid being. They grunted in surprise and a light snapped on in the corner in a quick reply.

'What are you doing here?' Hanuk spoke loudly and clearly. He held a lamp that was flickering and Celine couldn't see properly but had enough light for her well-adjusted eyes to see what was going on. The intruder was the male warrior who sat on the council. He looked sharply at Celine and then back at Hanuk. Reekei sat in the corner shadows and watched the exchange silently. She looked tired.

'I need to speak with you. It is very urgent.' The guest looked frantically at Hanuk and cautiously at Celine. Hanuk looked hard at Celine and spoke slowly.

'It is okay, say what you must in front of our guest and saviour.' The way he said 'saviour' made Celine believe he really didn't mean it at all. The toll of the last few days had taken a toll on the relationship here. She had not proved herself worthy and had failed at what, she was not sure.

'The council are deliberating the fate of the colony now. They are troubled with the state of the tribe above and are deciding what to do down here to counter the movement. They do not want to be in a weak position if something does happen. The king is losing favour and there is talk of an uprising.' The guard spoke quickly and surely. This news made the old man pause and even look enlivened.

'What can we do?' Asking as much himself, as the world around him. Celine got the feeling it was not an open question and kept silent. She looked at her guide and he looked back, her open face devoid of the disappointment of the day before. She sat up in what looked like a bed of animal skins woven together. Hanuk and the intruder looked comfortable and there was a clear level of intimacy they did not mind her seeing at this present moment.

Hanuk addressed the intruder.

'Tell the others on your way back to be ready. Tell the silent guard that there will be a moment to act and they will know it. Go now and be back before they notice you are gone. We must have the information you provide and your strength when the time calls. Thank you.' With that, the intruder reached out and grasped the forearm of the man and woman in turn. A slight tilt of the head to Reekei in what Celine would call a gesture of respect and he was off, brushing roughly past Celine and out into the night. Reekei rose and exited shortly after. She did not address Celine but lightly touched Hanuk on the arm and spoke softly to him.

'You know what must be done. Do not worry. I will be back soon.'

The darkness swallowed the guard deeply. She looked out into the passage and could not even tell which way he had gone. This place was creepy and seemed alive to her. She was not sure if she would call the mountain good or bad if asked and was even afraid to get to know it. She was called back softly by her guide and she sat down at the entrance to her sleeping space. Reekei whispered close to her ear the importance of keeping quiet and not mentioning this encounter to anyone. Celine was just glad the mood towards her had changed and was in agreement that she did not want to alter that situation if it kept her safer. She wanted to get out of there and was sure there would be pleasant and unpleasant ways to do that. There was a line to walk with how she handled the people. Her temper could make things harder than they needed to be. She knew that and she settled down back in her space, determined to play this game the right way.

66. Trudging

The mountain slipped by under the hands and feet of Daone. She climbed hand over hand down the shaft and into the belly of the mountain. It was colder down here than on the surface. It was dripping wet on the walls and it was as if the storm above was leaking down into the crevices of the mountain and threatening to wash it away. She wondered how far it would go down when it abruptly ended and a large room opened up around her feet. The wooden rungs ended suddenly after a curve in the tunnel levelled it out so she was climbing horizontally. She was tired and sore and just wanted to lie down now. The effects of the drugs, adrenaline and hype of seeing new people had worn off and she felt comfortable enough that she was not going to be murdered spontaneously from a dark corner. They had kept her alive and saved her from a worse fate above, so she could be a bit more hopeful with the outcome of the next little while. She was looking for a promising place to lie down and missed the male in black robes motioning her over to an offside tunnel. She was really done when she saw him waving his arms and his voice penetrated her senses. She followed, and it was good that she did, as he led her through to a small room with a warm fire glowing in the middle. There were five beds of rough looking material arranged around the fire to accommodate the most warmth. She was led to one of these, where she was handed a tough looking doughy bread, dripping in warm broth. Daone devoured this completely and promptly fell asleep sideways, with food still rolling around her mouth. She was exhausted and at the end of her tether. She slept soundly with her new friends around her, not caring if they were actually friends, but this was the best she'd had in ages. She curled up in her sleep, close to the fire, and the black robed leader covered her up. This was the start of something new and everyone around could feel it.

67. FITTING IN

Morning came after a long sleep for Daone. She didn't know it, but she had been asleep for a long time. She felt rested beyond her best sleep. This may have been her best sleep ever. She looked down and saw she had been bathed and her wounds taken care of by careful cleaning and a poultice mixture applied to them. This one was pinkish-yellow, the same colour as the clay around her. She was in new clothes as well and she was considering the food she'd been given might have been spiked as she did not remember any of this happening, as it must have been an invasive procedure. She also could have just been exhausted and that was what she was asleep for. She seemed to be in good working order and she was not bound or gagged. The environment did not feel hostile as she looked around at the group. The same two people as before were present, the black robed one and the guide who now looked much like the other one, as they were no longer covered in tribal paint and were as clean as she in their own set of black robes.

This was getting weird. The other occupant was a young female. Shorter than the others, she could have been mistaken for a child had she not looked so grown up and in place with the other two. If she had been seen above she would have assumed it was a child.

'What is going on here?' Daone asked. 'Why have you brought me here? I mean I don't mind and thank you for saving me as it wasn't very nice where I was. I am not ungrateful, just curious, what is going on?' It all fell out of her and she was speaking words one over the other in an attempt to get her point across. She had not spoken to many people lately and she needed this to go well. She did not want to have a repeat of the surface and she did not want to be sent back up there either. She doubted this last possibility as being likely as there seemed to be no love lost when coming down here. There did not seem to be any obvious connection between the two different peoples and she was happy to be guests of these ones.

'We are the Blue Tribe,' the small woman spoke. Her voice was soft and carried the air of being listened to without having to shout. Obviously her size was not a determining factor in rank. 'Why have you come here?'

'I... I did not choose to be here,' Daone replied. 'I was stranded here on the island. I didn't even choose this place. I was attacked in the boat by a woman, Celine, who is around the island somewhere I might add. Probably dead. So no, I did not choose this but here I am. That tribe tried to kill me, they are crazy and I hope you are not.'

It was as if she was coming to terms with the situation as she was speaking and her speech reflected that. She realised she must sound so dumb and wished she felt more together or knew more about what this was. She could usually read a room and say the right thing if she had more information, but she knew she had no idea what was going on here and did not want to come off rude or threatening. She looked from one to the other of the people and then the woman spoke again.

'You will come with us. We have your friend and you may be able to help sort out the situation we are in. We can't go into the city as normal but we have somewhere safe we can go and have her brought to you. Then we can get this all sorted out.' She turned to leave and Daone called after her.

'What, where is she? What city? What is going on?'

'We will tell you and show you, come.' She spoke in that same soft voice over her shoulder and Daone hurried on sore feet to catch up. The two others who'd come with her from the surface watched her go and conversed in quiet voices as she did.

'Weird, but still better than the alternative,' Daone thought and limped after this new Blue tribal member who commanded such respect from the room.

The tunnels were small. They were not made for a human of Daone's size and she had to combat the small space with a combination of crawling, stooping, and sliding through gaps to fit. The female leading her through had an easy enough time of moving through. The tunnels were cut for a person a bit bigger than her so she moved with a grace and flow that made Daone hurry to keep up. She was not given any more information as she went and had to mull over what she saw—which wasn't much—and what she had already learnt.

She knew there were at least two tribes here on the island, there could be more but it seemed unlikely as the size of the island meant there would be tough competition for everyone to exist without seeing the other. She knew they were relatively lucky where they'd landed, that they'd remained alone for so long. She did not see a particularly low point up ahead and knocked her face against the rough rock. She sighed as there was no slowing down from the woman ahead and not even an acknowledgement of anything happening. Daone kept on and just fell behind, her sore legs lagging and her spirits dampening at having to move this way for a long time. She was moving by the flicker of the lamp torch up ahead and the one held in her hands. The lights were making her tired, dancing across the space. At least here it was warming up and the blood was pumping back into her fingers and toes. She missed the fireside she had slept at for so long and the warm pile of blankets called to her. The tunnel wove ahead sharply and she lost sight of her guide. She rounded the corner and nearly ran into her. A large tunnel opened up behind them and was accessed by a small wooden door, opened out against the rock.

'This is where you will wait for me. I will return here by the end of this day with your friend.' She slipped through the door and shut it behind her. Daone was left alone, in the tunnel with a slowly dying torch. It would not last that long and she would have to shelter here, in the dark and cold. What kind of people were they, to save her and then leave her here to near freeze in this dark tunnel? Her back hurt and she lay down to stretch it out and think about things going on here. She needed a plan, she needed information and she was weary about seeing Celine. She did not know what type of relationship she had with these people and she did not want to be on the back foot as she had been with the other tribe. She was used to being in control and she could feel the urge to discredit Celine coming up so she could be seen as the golden... Whatever. Better than her. She was more valuable, she knew that through her more superior training and experience. Celine was as good as useless next to her and she just had to be ready to show everyone else that she was. She wondered how she would know when the 'day' was up, as it was not broadcast to her what time of day it was. Maybe they had other ways of measuring days and she would be shown that later too. She felt herself nodding off and it was almost as if the mountain was rocking her to sleep. She could have sworn she felt the mountain move and rumble, as if soothing her. The last memories she had were of the other tribe jeering at her and thoughts of how at least she was safer here, out of the weather. It might even still be raining.

68. Worrying

Reekei was not back and Hanuk was fretting. It was not like him to show this type of emotion. There had always been an assumed connection between the guide and her partner. They seemed to be on the same page with decisions and even if they were not it was obvious they were still connected throughout. You could tell they were connected but as two flames, dancing through their own lives. It must have been hard for them to remain so dedicated to their truth down here. Everyone else Reekei had met seemed content either to stay and live in hope of it getting better, or they were in charge and all they seemed intent on doing was keeping it that way. There was an obvious split between those who had the power and those who did not.

The sound of people outside their cave slice pulled Hanuk out of his worry. He caught Celine watching him and stood taller, pulled himself in and addressed her.

'I have to go,' he said. It was obvious why, but he did not mention it out loud to Celine. Either it was too hard to vocalise where his imagination was taking him right now or he crazily believed that Celine was not aware of his energy and actions and how weirdly he was acting and he thought she would actually believe what he was saying. She did hope that the guide was okay as she *had* been nice to her, even if she had ignored her after Celine had not done what she had wanted. But who could have blamed her? What was she even supposed to have done? Pushed past the council and broken them all out into the world to get beaten and possibly eaten by the Green Tribe? No, thank you. She had not made it this far to go down in some stupid soppy power play for these people, even though they had sort of taken her in and looked after her. Why couldn't she just be one of them, happy and content to stay down here and be safe? They had everything they needed to survive, and who needed to be out in the world where they could die? They were safer here. Celine would stay for now and then when the time was right, she would leave. Yes, that's right, she would leave and find her acquaintance and they would leave this sordid place. They might even get off this island alive and she could salvage some sort of life. Free somewhere else. It was such a plan and she didn't need these people ruining it for her. She was decided.

She watched Hanuk leave and he didn't even try to tell her not to go anywhere. Maybe all the care had gone out of them or they knew she wouldn't get far. Either way, she hunkered down next to the fire. She greedily put some more of the peaty substance on, not caring if there was some rule or limit to it. This was going to get better. No one had come and beaten her today and she was feeling great at being left alone. Maybe the guide should go missing more often, she thought.

69. Reuniting

The morning dragged for Celine. She was standing around the fire. Impatient. It had been too long since she had seen Reekei. Since she'd had instructions. Since she had been able to make decisions about where she was going to go and where she was going to escape to. She paced up and down in the room. Hanuk sat quietly in the corner. He had returned late without Reekei. He looked like he had a lot on his mind. He stared into the flames and patted his leg, as if in thought. It wasn't like the guide to be late or waste time. If Celine actually had power here and was actually needed for whatever cause they had, then she should be doing something. Not just sitting here. She was tensing up and her feet got heavier where they fell. The tension was building in the room. Unchanged, Hanuk stared just as calmly as before.

Relief found Celine when Reekei finally entered the chambers. She quickly walked in and spoke to Hanuk, also addressing Celine. Hanuk looked calmer with Reekei back but held back any overt gestures. He listened to her speak.

'We need you to come with us. We have someone for you to meet. We have the other one.'

Her ears pricked up at this. Daone. *They had the other one.* It could only be her troublesome partner. She turned her body to face the guide's back, stepped up to her and slammed her fist down onto Reekei's head. She stepped through the falling body and smashed two fists into Hanuk, who was still in the process of rising out of his seat. They winded him but he was still standing, still in the fight. He could not breath enough to yell for help though and the guide was out cold on the floor. She was not getting back up for a while but she was still alive and breathing. Celine took a moment and picked a point on Hanuk's head to aim at. She was still in a heightened state and was not thinking clearly about what her plan was, just that she needed to act. She was connected to another part of herself or something higher and that was what she was making decisions from. She swung high and knocked him in the forehead and he fell back into the wall behind him with a low thud. She paused for a moment to see if anyone would come and investigate this noise, and was greeted by no one as she stood there frozen. She stepped back to the guide and rifled through her robes. There was nothing in them and she realised she must do everything by memory. As if she would have a map or anything that gave away where she could navigate to in the mountain and beyond. She must be a lot older than she looked to hold such a mountain of information. Very competent.

Reekei did not lay unconscious for long after Celine had left. She stirred and after the shock of seeing Hanuk laid out before her subsided, checked to make sure he was okay. She left him laying there to wake on his own and set off to exact her wrath on the unfolding situation.

70. Rising

The sun rose over the mountain. The rain had stopped and the island looked different. The water had washed away a lot of the banks surrounding the river, as if a great flood had taken the nearest water's edge and clawed away at the sand. There was a deep indent where the water had eroded the edge and some of the tribe's tents had been washed into the water and taken far downstream. Some had drowned and some had made it out alive, left to defrost and dry out far from help and their community. They wandered aimlessly on the shores where the water receded back into the main river system and picked at random items strewn about. The tribe would send out people to look for those lost. They were valuable in numbers and would need to find them.

It was only a small portion who had the unfortunate status to be in such a precarious home. They had places assigned on status and what they brought to the tribe. Tanners and builders were very important as they supplied many items and services for the camp. Warriors were also given high ranks. Lower classes like the tent from which the uprising was whispered about were some of those to get swept away.

The young boy who'd spoken so wildly about changing the status quo of the tribe was covered head to toe in mud and was slopping his way through the slimy residue left on the shore. His feet squelched and stuck as he lifted them, keeping an eye out for items useful to him and an ear out to hear of anyone in the area who might need his help. He was not a fan of the status system that kept him so far away from the ambitions that painted his dreams. This was not the life he had planned for himself and he was aware of the change he hoped to bring about in the tribe. He was not the only one. He had spoken to enough old people who wanted more to change and more of the old ways to return. There were even some young people who were not happy, and they had known no different. His stories spurred a fight in them for a better way. They were tired and alone. Well, they felt that way. They had people around but it was rare to find someone they could talk to, to connect with and share their dreams and wants with. There were people a plenty, but they only had space for the talk the Medicine King spread. It was as if they had one voice and one eye. All they saw and all they spoke about was someone else's vision with someone else's words. Anything outside of that was seen as a threat and squashed with violence, manipulation and fear. Who wanted to be kicked out of the tribe for being different and who wanted to be strung up by their ankles and hung from the cliffs? All these things had happened as an example to others to fall into line and accept how things were. Even so, the conversations had started and the whispers could be heard in the right circles. There was change in the air and he was here for it. He lost himself in his work. Dreaming of the future and repeating the monotonous task of picking up his life out of the mud and pulling it all together again.

When the waters receded, the lookouts from the Blue Tribe informed the council. They were a special section of the tribe that was separated and lived between the council chambers and the outside world. There were no families here. They were all devoted in singularity to the council and the tribe and were fanatic in that approach. They did what they were told, when they were told. Part of their role was to watch the outside world at certain points and report back any events or to keep daily eyes on the island from the safety of the mountain. They did this via a series of tunnels and eye holes cut into the rocks overlooking the green Serpunt tribe. This was a special role and it was seen as an honour to be chosen to perform it.

The current lookout over the camp was standing at his post, eyes glued to the outside and not looking around him for fear of missing an important going-on. He did not hear the person sneak up behind him and slit his throat. There was no kindness in the action. He was not caught and lowered to the ground out of anything other than the necessity that the sound of him falling could give away his perpetrator to another lookout. His eyes rolled slowly back into the rear of his head and his last gurgling breath allowed him to see his attacker step over his slowly dying body and head further, deeper into the caves. There was danger entering the cave system, in the long winding passageways of the life of the Blue Tribe. There was danger coming and no one was going to warn them until it was too late.

71. Change

The mountain woke everyone like normal. The hustle and bustle of the mountain tribespeople went about business as usual. They got to work, gathering the peaty resource they found underground. Refining it and passing it up the chain of production until it was good enough to pass out to the families and communities who depended on it for warmth and cooking. The oil reserves that were distilled to light the lamps and torches grew. The food supplies were eaten and restocked. The chosen gatherers went out and acquired what they could while remaining hidden. These were another special breed. They were as loyal—if not more—as the guards; the watchers on the cliff.

Silence was the council's best ally. Having loyal people who were invested in the survival of the tribe. Who worked unchecked and could be trusted to be cunning and savage to align the outcomes of the day with the outcomes of the council, disguised as the outcomes of the tribe. It was they who ventured out to the base of the cliffs by the sea, to the forests way beyond the Blue Tribe and gathered the most precious plants for healing and care. It was weird that they were not missed from the night shift, where they used the cover of the darkness to complete their plans. The special quarters they inhabited were empty and yet no one had raised any alarm. It was because the watchers and lookouts were not there to raise an alarm. They were all strewn about the base of the cliff. Pushed out from their crevices. Dragged to the top soil and left strangled and slit where wild animals could and had been feeding on them. Their hopes and dreams for the tribe were dashed and their role was left empty. The watchers and lookouts were replaced with mute warriors, painted blue over green. A harsh contrast and mixture of the two tribes. A blending of one with other. The Blue Tribe did not know this yet, they were not aware that death had come to the mountain.

72. Stocking

T hings were not going well for Reekei. She was cold and scared and slammed into a small space, standing upright. She already could not feel her toes as they dangled down into the water. The cold seeped in and the heat and feeling seeped out. This was not good, but she didn't know what to do about it. She could not stop thinking about her dear Hanuk. He would not understand this. To lose her would break him and he was kind of heart, even if he did not show it to other people much. He loved her very much and that love is what she kept coming back to in the dire situation she was in. She kept snapping herself out of this comforting thought as she knew that was the place she would go before the end, before she gave up living and transferred over into the realm of the gods. She kept pulling herself away from those thoughts and knew she did not want to go yet. She wanted—no *needed*—to stay in the land of the living and see this through. She had not come this far with her love, had not come this far with her people, to be squashed out of life and left to die in this small crevice in the rock.

It was not really a crevice. This was more of a store room, small and unobtrusive. There were many dotted over the mountain complex as they stored a lot of what was used and survived on down here. She knew there were caches and other storage places the tribe used on the island, not that she was meant to. She was often seen as quiet, even shy to the townspeople, and even the council. It was not that she had nothing to say, it was that she knew it would fall on dead ears. She was speaking loudly with her actions, being the head of a rogue group of people who wanted change on the island. They were all together in the fight for freedom and she knew when to stay quiet and when her actions spoke volumes. She was adept at being invisible in crowds, blending in with the forest, and so she had been able to find these hidey-holes and deposits of supplies. She was even able to go in and find the very hidden things that not even some of the top members of the council were aware of. This access was granted by her knowledge of people. She knew who to speak to for what, what made them tick and who to avoid completely if they could not be swayed or if they were too volatile to trust. The key was predictability. The more predictable a person was, even if that predictability was horrible, disgusting and vile, the more she could work with them. People had patterns and once you learnt them, there were only a certain amount of ways you could play those people.

She was a trusted accomplice of the council. She was not a member, far from it, but she was what they appreciated. One of the people and could be seen as walking among them, she could disappear into them and spend long amounts of time with them, listening. She could do this and report to the council what was going on, who was saying what and what the general consensus of the people was. She knew there were others who had similar roles as her, but no one was like her. Being able to hear both sides to the story she was able to manipulate what was passed on, protect the people who were most valuable to her and target those who were a threat to her cause. This trust was how she had been given the job of finding the saviour. She knew the council would want to control the narrative as much as possible and to do that they needed access to the gold.

This person was set to come to them on this moon and change the lives of everyone. The whole mountain was talking about it and the lucky ones had gathered in the main chamber and joined in ritual for the coming. It was the guide who had been sent out to find this great one and bring them back. She was sent out, adorned in the tribal and ritual wear of her people. She looked different and she knew it. She'd had long robes of white, a headpiece and sandals strapped to her feet. She had changed with a hidden lot of clothes on the way out. She was not going to go out and be such a target for herself with the Snake Tribe out on this night too. They had heard the speaking of light, the same as all the others. That this one would come and save them. They would be out looking for this person. The golden one. And the guide had found them. She had been hiding behind a rock, having followed the two women as they had snuck through the bushes up the mountain. They had been loud and the guide had thought this was a bad start. They were going to be found anytime soon and this would all be over. Being taken by the Snake Tribe was a death mark. She was thinking her plan was all going to fail when luck struck. They had separated. The loud one had stayed behind and a soft footed Celine had run down the track towards her. She had acted instinctually and reached out her hand and energy to motion her over. It was smooth and easy after that. Celine had not been bothered about leaving her friend and came with her easily. The robes were still hidden out on the track from the caves but she had snuck away when she had entered the main cavern so no one had been any wiser about her changed plan. She was weary of the council already, but it comforted her that they had plans to make this saviour fail. This would be at the expense of herself. If she was captured and killed, there would be no one to find the saviour.

Reekei was reliving these last couple of days and the events leading up to this. To be alone and stuck, with no plan to escape. The cold seeped up her legs and took more of her. She was reverse melting into the icy water. Her body became more with the mountain. Time went on and her internal journey continued. She was met with her own mortality. The rock ground into her back, each small movement was torture. Each breath was a labour. The love of her people brought her back again and again. From the edge of letting go she returned to the small crevice-like cave in the rock and the pain of defeat.

The mountain shook and woke her. She had nodded off and it was hard to believe as she was so cold and numb. She was surprised she'd had any comfort to find here by sleeping. Images of the men who'd put her in here flashed over and over again in her mind's eye. They were violent and swept through the outer stages of the mountain's defence. The watchers and the ones who lived on the edge. They watched the mountain. The passes and the passages that led to the depths and the heart. The mass of people who lived in the mountain. They were reliant on it. They sourced their water, fuel, warmth, food and their comfort from it. It provided safety from the outside world. It sheltered them from the massive storms that ravaged the island for half the year. The rain beat down on them but there was nothing to feel or fear in the mountain. It rocked on constantly. The rhythmic shaking that signalled day and night for those who dwelled beneath. It had kept them safe when so many had perished when the Green Tribe rose up.

Their evil ways had been evident for a while and the night it all came to a head, many thousands had died. It was a scar on their memories, those who could remember. Many had been born in hiding, in the mountain. It was home to them and they had never been outside or seen the sun or the moon. The cold mornings where the frost sat on the edge of her nose, or the hot period where she'd sat soaked in her own self until she got sick of it and cooled off in the rivers and waterholes. She knew what it was like to be free and she would never settle for this life that she had been given. There was always a light she was moving towards and this crevice would not be the end for her.

She could feel the tears welling up inside her as she took in the hopelessness of her situation. She was stuck in here, having stepped in to hide from the killing. They swept in with swords drawn and sliced the throats of them all. They all lay dead as she slipped in here. It was a place she had known about and she thought she was doing the smart thing by stepping in here. But she'd been seen. One of the men opened the door and showed his fellow murderers in the night what lay inside. They had all laughed to each other and made a decision to spare her for now. It was really prolonging her death and signing her to one of infinite more cruelty and pain.

She was standing upright with blades poking in all around her. As soon as she moved one way or the other a blade would stick her. She had already sliced a hole in her arm when she'd faltered earlier and hadn't stayed upright. She had slipped on the cold rocks beneath the water and the pain had jolted her back awake. She could not move, or death would seize her but the instinct to not die was keeping her still. She could not see a way out of this and her hands were cut where she'd tried moving blades or shifting herself. At least the cuts went numb pretty soon as the draft was harsh here. She was impressed at the builders of the labyrinth of tunnels, as some were kept at a reasonable temperature and some connected by shafts to the surface were able to be kept quite cool. The tears started in earnest now as the loneliness took her. A deep sob shook her body and a cut opened up along her lower back on the right. She sucked in air quickly stopping her body moving and silently moved through the emotion until she was left stone-like. Too afraid, too lost to move. She silently waited out her inevitable end and thought of her Hanuk.

73. Pain

Water trickled down the walls in the small cave where Reekei was trapped. It was more like an alcove with a door. A crude door at that. The wooden panels were shoved into the bedrock. Sharp edges gripped the tough rock. She assumed she was imagining the sound when she heard it. The soft pull of recognition dragged her from her foggy state.

The sound continued even though she was awake. Great, now she was hallucinating. But no, the sound continued. The light changed in her small upright coffin. The light entered in chunks of flickering firelight. The small splotches of light stung her eyes. She instinctively shut them and soothed her eyes with the darkness she found there.

'Reekei, Reekei, it's me.' She opened her eyes a sliver and saw Hanuk reach in and grab for her before she fell into him. Her sweet, sweet Hanuk. How did he find her and what is going to happen to them? This was not the future she'd envisioned for them.

The colony was in grave danger and all she could do was fall. She lay slumped in his arms as he gently laid her out on the floor. The people around him stepped forward and took the prone figure.

'We will take her from here, sir.' Reekei was carried away. Two of the four carried and two remained with Hanuk. They set off deeper into the tunnels, the opposite direction to his partner. This was war and he was not going to let this action ruin him or his plans. Revenge and success would go hand in hand for him.

Hanuk had fallen into line too many times in his life. He was around at the original turn of the tribes. He had stood by and seen his family ripped apart. He had done nothing to stop the powers of the council; ripping apart the tribes and installing in them a new hierarchy of power, a new hierarchy of living that saw them cowering in the caves like wild animals, and scared ones at that. The squashing of power that had occurred over the years had built a fortress of hate, a fortress of resentment for himself. He blamed himself for not doing anything by going along with the plan of others. Who was he to say anything if he thought something was wrong? There were people in a place of power for a reason; to look after the tribe. But the power had been controlling these members of the council for a long time. It had built to a point where they could dictate the movements of the tribe. They served the council with their lives and instead of having the council exist for the people and serving them, they were squashed here underground. Waiting to die as slaves, cut off from their lifeblood, the land.

They'd lived before. They were connected to the seasons. They were connected to the moon and the changing of the tides that licked at the beaches and then, when they were torn away from it, the sand and rocks lay bare for them to walk on. They saw and experienced the raw strength of the wind and rain, pummelling them for a season and threatening to wash them all away. But they had none of this now. They had 'safety'. From the outside world and from the Green Tribe. This enemy who was so great and so deadly that they could not risk facing them.

He was sure there was some foul play. He had thought it back then and he definitely thought it now. He knew it now. He was connected with spies in the high council chambers. He had ears that stretched around corners and eyes that peered into cracks as thin as a fingernail. The thing that came with 'safely' pushing a whole tribe and expanse of people underground is that they'd squished out the space. There were opportunities to put people in everywhere and Hanuk was good at people. He came across as quiet, even shy and uninterested, but he was not. He listened more than he spoke and he saw more than what people wanted him to. He could find the pivot point with someone. The thing that connected them to their heart and made them stop. He drew out the best in people alone and in groups so well that he had organised a resistance. A group dedicated to finding the truth of what lay beneath, beneath this enslavement to the mountain and its rulers. He was at the head of a vast organisation of the tribes and he was at a pivotal moment. It was all coming to a head.

The meeting of the tribes was upon them. They would have justice and he would have his redemption. He ploughed on further into the tunnels, keeping alert for the slightest sound out of place. His senses were heightened and his eyes adjusted to the flickering light of his torch and the darkness around. He could hold his torch at an angle where it lit up the tunnel but didn't blind him to the cracks and darkness to his sides. He would not be jumped, he would not be snuck up on.

He came to a forking of the tunnels and chose one that rose slightly off to his left. There were many curves and turns that swung him back and forth until he could hear soft voices up ahead. He slowed his pace and prepared for a confrontation up ahead. He put his torch down slowly on the ground, out of eyesight, and took the last steps to make it to the edge of the light up ahead. He could hear the soft padding of the two warriors' footsteps he had brought with him on his quest. Their presence was comforting, as they had been with him since the beginning and could be trusted implicitly. One last inhale, feeling their presence around him, then he stepped out into the light of the widening corridor before him.

74. Fighting

Celine was anxious. She was not sure where she was going. She had a fair idea and the people and caves she passed looked familiar. It was a labyrinth down here and the number of people packed into such a small area surprised her. It was weird she was noticing this now, on the cusp of her escape. She kept her head down and moved on. It was a futile attempt at not bringing attention to herself, but as the only full-sized human here, it was a lost cause. She still didn't raise too much attention as she had been around a while now and they had grown used to seeing her a bit. It was far quieter than when she had first arrived. She would have been mobbed by young and old to tell her story or stand up against a wall to measure how tall she actually was.

The caves started to get dingier and she knew she was reaching the area she had been looking for. It was more dangerous, she felt but safer in a way as there was less care here, and more 'anything goes' attitude. She skimmed around some boulders and leftover wooden buckets strewn haphazardly in the middle of the path, then stepped through a doorway that almost looked hidden, as if the rock was meant to cover the slot, keeping it looking more natural and less inviting to go into. It was what was on the other side of this rock that had her attention.

A man had sat out in the main walkway and stared at her whenever she'd passed with the guide. She had not passed without her, so it was every time. This had been her experience of him and she had felt there was more here than what was being shown and told to her. She wanted to speak to this man, hear his story and see if he could help her escape. The tension in her was building as the small waiting room opened up before her.

'What do you want?' boomed a voice from a room beyond. The next room opened up quickly and she stepped into the living quarters of an actually well-off and tidy person. It wasn't as if they had no possessions, but they were arranged and organised. Care had been taken to make the space seem sparse, but 'neat' was what came across to Celine. She stood looming over the man she was looking for and was shocked by his appearance. He stood tall and met her gaze with level eyes. It was as if he was amused at seeing her here and was not fussed at having a guest or intruder in his home. Celine looked down at the man standing on his ledge and was at a loss for words.

'I don't understand,' she said. 'When I've seen you...'

'People see what they want to see,' he replied, cutting her off before she could pause to think of a word. 'The world goes past and makes assumptions about me. About how I look, my cleanliness, my dress. What they fail to realise is that it is an act. A way of hiding in plain sight and it is me who watches them. I see and hear things that they would be surprised to hear themselves. There is an abundance of loose tongues down here and shadowed eyes.'

75. Stupor

Daone was cold, wet and hungry. She felt like she had been battered and bruised and her feet were so cold she thought they would fall off soon. The room she was in was dank. The water pooling around her feet was rancid and stale. It had not moved except when she shivered uncontrollably and shuffled it around a bit. The room had a cold breeze that flowed through it intermittently. It stopped and she thought she was regaining some heat, and then it returned, billowing around her and stealing any of the warmth from her pockets like candy from a baby. She didn't know how these things had come to pass. One minute she was with friends. She had been taken care of and bathed. She had been fed and left to sleep. It did not make sense that she would then be treated like this. It made no sense. That is what she kept telling herself.

There were new players afoot in her digs. They wore all black and stank of stale fish. Not as bad as the room, but bad in their own right. It was the smell of death that hung about them. Breathing through their pores as she'd been thrown in here, it got on her skin, etched in her brain, the smell of her own end. This would surely have to be her end. How many lives did she have? How many times could she be found by someone and taken in? She knew she hadn't had an overly lucky life but it had had its moments, surprising her with its ups. She knew she'd had so many downs, but it was the ups that she held onto. The evidence of hope in her life that made her matter. She mattered so much to someone or something that things went right. The ship was an example of that.

She'd been at a loss in the port, wandering after having spent all her money gambling. She even had debts. People were after her. Men with long memories and short fuses. They would come for her and take their pay in cash or other. She'd known that and all she could do was give up and wander the port. She wasn't sure what to do and she looked for a way out in every store window and down every alley. This was what she was doing when fate found her. She had ambled down a particularly dank alley, not as dank as this place, but not far off. The rubbish in the drains held up the water flowing away and made it smell and rot. She was looking into a rather dusty and cluttered store that sold rugs and other imports strewn about over the place. Not really a place for things but organised to seem like it was meant to be there, in its random placing. She'd heard footsteps behind her and thought this must have been the men coming to collect. But this was different. These men didn't usually travel alone. It was not safe for them. They did not make friends in the town and it was easier to collect against one when there were more of them to do the collecting. This was one set of steps coming closer to her. Some steps were clear on the cobblestones, others muffled by the strewn debris.

'I've come to offer you an option,' the voice said. It was clear of any slurs or anger. Nothing aimed at her besides the words and their meaning. No undercurrent of malcontent.

'A choice of what?' she asked. Without turning, she closed her eyes and thought about running anyway. What good could this bring? But where would she go? There was no hiding from the people here and to leave through one of the gates of the city would trigger an even worse fate for her. Word would spread and she would be hunted down. No, she would stay and hear what this person had to say and decide if it would benefit her in the least. She didn't need much, just the bare minimum and its way of biding her over until the next hurdle her life threw at her.

'An option,' he repeated. 'I will pay your debt and you come and work for me.'

Well now, a way out and a job, things are looking better,' she thought. She slowly turned around and stared into the eyes of what could be her new employer.

'Why would you give me a job?' she asked. Not, 'Why would you pay my debt,' that wasn't as outlandish as it would seem. This man had the looks of being quite wealthy and while her debts were crushing and life threatening to her, they would be loose change thrown to a beggar on the street compared to the really wealthy. No, to employ someone meant that there was a vision of a benefit for them and she wanted to know what that was. How cheaply was she selling her soul?

'A job on a boat,' he had answered. 'I need some cargo transported across the sea and I've seen the way you hold yourself. I see something in you and have uses for such things.' She creased up her eyebrow at this but pushed no further on the matter. Whatever this man thought he saw, in a pub, in a brawl, in passing, was nothing to her. There was a job and she would do it. This was her way out of this situation and she would grab it with both hands. In hindsight it might have paid to ask more questions, but who would have known? This was her with her back against the wall. This was her way out.

'When and where do you need me?'

From there things had been easy. The debt was paid and she was free to gamble and drink in whichever pub suited her. That was only for a day, as the ship she was due to set sail on was to leave port the next day. She had minimal time to get her things together and she was given personal provisions on the ship. Things like clothes and a personal portion of rum and gin. These she kept in her tiny cabin.

The ship was a deep, dark creature of a thing. Twists and turns criss-crossed the hull. Three storeys of holds flanked by cabins for crew and others. She was not sure about these 'others' or the cargo. It was already loaded when she was aboard. The 'others' she was told about and told not to go looking around below deck. Things would all be explained once out to sea. So she'd waited and was sucked into her new job and her new opportunity at life.

76. Salvation

This was hard. This whole life had been hard. Celine did not know when she'd had a moment of ease in this life. She didn't know if she'd had an easy life in last life either and this was to make up for it. It didn't really matter either way. This was all she knew and she was getting sick of it. It almost made her want to give up. Again and again she found herself in this position, where the world felt against her. She felt like she had no one and no support. She was alone, that she was sure of. If she was going to get out of this mess she was going to have to do it alone. Hanuk was not going to save her. She barely knew the guy and he was storming through the caves and tunnels below the mountain killing every council guard he saw and making them answer with blood.

She had gotten swept up in the killing. The blood of her captives stained her hands red. She was buying time, she knew. The moment she was no longer of value to this resistance would be the moment she would be gone, piled high into the bodies that lined the walls.

Written down as a part of this story that was there; played a part but did not do much. Was not a main character and did not contribute meaningfully. She was sure she was only a main character in her own story. She would not even be interested in hearing her own story. What a sad collection of affairs. To be stood and trodden on in different environments. Different place, still a shit situation. This was her life. She swung her arms and the wooden club spiked with barbs splattered and squashed anything that got in its way. This was her life. Slowly ebbing away from her and into this mountain and its story.

77. RAGING

Hanuk was angry. He was aflame with madness and he could not seem to pull himself back from the edge. The pain he had felt and kept shut inside him over the last years had eaten away at him. This was the release he had been waiting for. The pain was being spread over all those he came in contact with. The ones who resisted were dealt misery in every blow until they could feel no more and he could move onto the next victim of his pain. There were those he left alone. The ones who had helped him or the resistance. They wouldn't even know there was such a major resistance building over the years and they had still helped him.

78. Delivering

The mountain was awash with activity. Celine was swinging the club she had acquired from the mysterious watcher in the tunnels. It looked like a rougher area and it was. She had spoken to the stranger briefly. She was at the end of her tether and he could feel it. He knew she had come to him at the right time. The prophecy had spoken of the saviour. What others did not know was that he could speak to the mountain. He knew her ways and was privy to the specifics of today. He could decipher what it said. *Speak to her.*

He knew Celine was coming to save them and deliver them to the surface once more. It did not have to be in the way the council expected it to happen. In stifling her efforts and ability to fight for them, they had led her down the path she was truly meant to go. It was from this chaos that had bubbled up that Celine would be able to operate and let go enough of her old self to step into who she really was. He'd told her briefly that this was her truth and handed her the bludgeoning tool made from a special and sacred tree that used to grow up on the mountain. After the Blue Tribe was forced to flee underground, the tree was burnt by the Serpunt tribe, but this remained. It was made of the land and a piece of the mountain and island. It would now be wielded by their hero and vanquish them of the council, freeing the tribe. Off Celine had gone and now there was a lot of killing going on. She had it in her head that she would be going out to hunt the Serpunt tribe and on the way she had run into lots of them, roaming the tunnels nearest the exit. The chill of feeling safe when they really hadn't been ran down her spine, then the thrill at getting to actually do something to direct her own life hit her. So, she hit them. It was on!

79. Revenge

The dripping from the cave ran down the walls around Hanuk as he stalked the tunnels leading to the council chambers. He had been wandering the edge of the mountain. He was clearing the tunnel of the intruder guards whom he had suspected had been let in by the council. He was heading there now to confront them and get some answers. Answers or blood. He was not sure yet if he would spare them. He had been bloodlusted for much of the morning, since finding his beloved Reekei stuffed into a small chamber lined with spikes. He wanted to inflict similar damage on those responsible. Celine was in a frenzy of her own. After attacking himself and Reekei, he'd been told she'd had a magnificent bat made from the sacred tree of the mountain. What a fitting weapon to use today, to shed some blood in the mountain. He kept pacing strongly and purposefully down the corridor, stopping every now and then to slay another guard who'd come to discover where his comrades were.

80. Brutalising

Celine swung the bat. *Spat.* The sound of the blood hitting the wall. *Crunch.* The sound of her weapon splitting yet another skull.

'This is a meditation,' she thought. She was not used to enjoying this so much. She had an expectation this would be hard and she would struggle but no, she took to this like a duck to water. This is what she was made to do and she was a killer. She was quite good at it and started varying her aim and swing to gauge if she could become more efficient with different techniques and methods. Further and further she ventured, not caring where she was going and paying little attention to the doors and corridors she went down.

The mountain was a mess. It was strewn with belongings and the dead. Thankfully, it was mostly Serpunts and only some guards from the Blue Tribe. Most of the common citizens from the mountain had barred themselves in their homes and chosen to ride this out from behind their closed doors. She knew some had fled, she guessed down to the river pools that ran under the mountain. That was where she would head in this situation. She did not know if there was a way out but it offered the biggest space besides the cloud room, which she'd come through into the mountain. She knew that room would be a poor option as it was heavily guarded by the council. She was almost unaware of her thoughts as she pressed on, swinging her bat. On and on, away from what she knew, which was very little already. Until she came to a small door set into the rock that looked unused and dirty. It was weird; it caught her eye as a deception. A purposefully dirty door that had been used recently as the scuff marks in the dirt gave it away. She pushed through, leveraging her bat to open the door from a distance, checking there was not someone waiting to inflict some of the same damage she was handing out. It was dark on the other side and she stepped through. She was shocked and angry to see Daone sitting in a corner huddled up and coming out of a sleep.

81. Hanging

The water on the cave walls flowed less and less as Hanuk approached the council chambers. He pulled himself up outside the entrance and nodded briefly with the two other assailants he had brought with him. They were fashioned in similar garb and tackle as him. They had come to fight. To lay waste to the parasite that was strangling this mountain. They stepped through one after the other and took in the scene that was waiting for them on the other side.

It was a bloodbath. The scene made what had been happening in the tunnels look like a kids party. The council were all hung, strung up by their elbows around the room. It looked as if they had been broken like animals ready to butcher. Their arms hung at odd angles, though something irked Hanuk, making the picture look strange and out of place. Arms snapped at the elbow, held together only by the flesh and used to support the weight of the members.

The scene did not quell Hanuk's rage. He was immune to this horrific experience he stood in the middle of. It seemed everyone who had held a spot at the table had been given a similar fate. One pile of golden robes lay huddled on the floor over by an exit door that led closer to the outside of the mountain. A slight stir made them all jump into alert mode, but they were just being wary. The pile could not harm them as the occupant was in a similar state as the rest. Being left on the ground meant more of the blood was still in her body than on the floor, and she still had a faint glow of life left in her. Her legs and arms had been fashioned in the same state and her eyelids hung heavy as she slipped in and out of consciousness.

'Who did this?' Hanuk spoke with such a lack of emotion, even with what had happened around them. It was not even registering as a tragedy or something to get upset about. It had happened and it was just another 'thing' on the way to his ultimate goal: The mountain's Blue Tribe freed and him, Hanuk, back with his Reekei. Silence hung in the air as the question was absorbed and a reply was given.

82. Surprising

Everything hurt. They had come out of nowhere. She still couldn't believe it. The Royal Guard, they'd done this. They had slit and broken and hung the whole council. She had watched as they went around the room, methodically performing the task. When they had gotten to her they had realised her arms would not support the position they had been putting the bodies into. This was a small blessing for her as she was subsequently broken and left on the floor.

'Was I that bad a servant to the people?' she thought. She knew she was lying to herself though. She was so close to the end and it felt like more weight to keep the lie going than free herself now. What had been created was not of the people's best interest, it was for hers and the other members. They had been acting out of fear for a while when the opportunity and threat from the Serpunt tribe had flared up. It was draining, holding onto this for so long. She was ready to be gone when a disturbance from across the room told her someone had entered.

An old man with two youngsters, poorly dressed but capable looking. They noticed her and she remembered them talking to her.

83. Reflecting

The walls felt like they were melting around her. The water running down the rock displaced the clay and ran brown. This was unusual, even for Daone who had seen quite a lot by now. She was put off sleeping as she was wary of the what-ifs going through her head. She sat and thought about her life here on the mountain. These opportunities she'd had at forging a friendship with Celine and her reluctance—over and over—to lean into that relationship. She knew, looking back, that there were times when she could have used that relationship more, like on the ship and having someone to talk to. They did work well as a team here and had natural strengths that complimented the other's. What they couldn't seem to get right was how stubborn they both were. They both had no willingness to relax into the other making decisions. Into the other leading for long periods of time. Even to their own detriment, they had to be in control and make decisions. This, it seemed, was their biggest downfall. She pondered this until the light from her torch grew fainter and fainter and she was eventually enveloped in the darkness of the cave. Even the melting sensation was no longer bothering her. She was suspended in time, it felt. She knew she would just wait until the guide came back, maybe things could be different with Celine now.

The door burst open and Daone was momentarily in shock to see Celine standing, panting, waving a long piece of a branch. The yelling seemed over the top to Daone's peaceful vigil. She didn't even feel offended or attacked despite the aggressive tone of delivery.

'What are you doing here?'

'I was told to wait here and you were going to be brought here. The woman told me so.' The way in which Daone delivered her reply seemed to diffuse all the tension out of the room. She did not react, did not bite at the fierceness delivered to her. She was simply stating the natural truth of it. No more, no less.

'Oh.' A noticeable droop of the shoulders told her that Celine was tired of fighting, here and with others. The weight of carrying herself and her direction, fighting everyone, hit her and she just did not have the space to fight Daone now too. She knew the mountain was in turmoil and here Daone was sitting in a dark room waiting for her.

'Fine, fine.' She said levelly. 'We had better go.'

84. Reckoning

The whole mountain shook. The inhabitants inside and outside knew it was a time of reckoning. Hanuk led his troop through the royal chambers and out into the sun of the island. It had been so long for him. Many, many seasons stuck underground. His eyes took time to adjust and he stood feeling the tremors underfoot. He could also hear people coming up the mountain. He looked around him; it was a small clearing with a rock face gradually heading up behind him. A large flat piece of rock that he had stepped out from behind melded into the larger rock, making the entrance invisible. Off in front of him, thick thorny bushes above head height wove away from him. He could see where a section had been hacked to make a slight tunnel that could take one creature at a time. A row of green war-painted Serpunt Tribe streamed into the clearing. It was clear to him that these were the ones responsible for the chaos in the caves, as the first handful were covered in blood. It was hard to look and find a stretch of skin not covered by either war paint or blood, that was the extent of their dedication to their cause.

Hanuk stood his ground and gave a level gaze to the new occupants of the space. He could feel the others bristle at this new development, waiting on a cue from him. He spoke in his normal language. He remembered when the tribes were whole and they'd all lived together.

'Who do we have to thank for the work there?' he said, motioning behind him. The leader, a smaller adolescent, looked up from behind green and red rimmed eyes.

'It waaaas me.' He drew out the word like it was a challenge. As if he was not yet sure why he was being thanked. Hanuk acknowledged this young warrior and spoke directly to him, on his level, even though he was many seasons his senior.

'We have been separated for too long. We do not wish to languish below any longer. We wish to rejoin under the sun and spend our time out here. What do you say to this?'

The young one thought to himself. It was unusual to have this type of conversation. At the end of a very long pause, he smiled up at Hanuk.

'We want this too. We have too long been subjugated by our own tribe. We wish to upheave the whole system. I do not want to live with my family under the King any longer. Will you help us kill him?'

The prospect at more revenge and bloodlust excited Hanuk. He also knew it would be good for the formation of the tribes if the leaders across both, who had orchestrated the separation, were both wiped out. The logic behind it was second to his deep desire to kill. He agreed wholeheartedly and the band of rebels formed up and set off for the king.

85. Freedom

Celine and Daone walked through the halls of emptiness. Celine was taking them to the council chambers. She was getting out and taking Daone with her. This had been enough. She was coming down off her killing high and there was little to stoke the fire in here. The Blue tribe were basically platonic and it was the combination of the council and the guards that were the real threat.

She was shocked, walking through the carnage of the horror-filled chamber. Daone was grey faced and ashen. Celine had seen the product of her own fury and anger and felt amazed at the level of destruction here. The blood trail led outside and she followed, leaving her own bloody footprints in the sand.

86. Frenzy

Hanuk and his merry band rounded a bend in the path, leading them up the mountain. As they did, they were met with the eyes of many a green Serpunt warrior. They were spread out across the path and into the clearing, where the King looked down on them from upon a large boulder.

'What do you want?' he screamed out in his shallow and haunting tone. The Serpunt warriors did not take their eyes from Hanuk's group, just making shallow hissing noises in their throats. They waved back and forth, trancelike. The mountain rumbled. Its quiet slumber seemed to rise and all took notice.

'We are here for the King—no longer. You are dead.' Hanuk motioned a slice across his own throat with his knife; a symbol the Serpunt King was enraged by. The thought of having his authority challenged sent him and his warriors into a frenzy and they charged the small group.

The Serpunt Tribe slammed into the collaborative group in an explosion of energy. Hanuk and his band formed a protective knot and fought back even more savagely. The Serpunts lost lives, falling down and being trodden on by their brothers and sisters from behind. The King laughed and sang his muddled spells. The group was surrounded and it was obvious they had no way out. Not one of them seemed to care.

The mountain revved up in an angry turbulence. The earth split down the side of the group. Many of the Serpunts were stranded and had to head off to try and find a way around. The King was unperturbed, screaming and singing incantations. He seemed to think the mountain was working in his favour and his voice was having an effect on the outcome.

87. Death

Celine was back in her zone. She swung the branch in front of herself, keeping her shoulder warm. She could hear a commotion up ahead and strode off the path around a boulder that was seemingly blocking the path up ahead.

'What are you doing?' Daone enquired.

'This way,' she ordered and kept moving. It was decided with not much work or words now what the action path was. Celine was leading and moving and Daone could keep up or drop off. She was in no mood to be left again and kept watch all around, keeping an ear on the commotion.

The path led up the mountain and was narrow and edged with thorns. They came to a boulder overlooking the mass of the tribes and the culprits of the noise. She could see the Serpunt King's back, his hands waving and war cries penetrating the sky. The Serpunts were attacking what looked like a band of their own and surprisingly... Hanuk. He was in the middle of a group flanked by two others from the caves, the Blue Tribe. He was fighting ferociously. Celine was surprised to see how changed he looked. He was alive with the fight and frightening to watch.

The carnage was staggering. The small group were fighting back but in vain. The more they killed, the more stepped up the slope to replace those lost. The rage grew in Celine. She watched the killing and the death all around. It took her back to the boat and the misery she'd experienced there. As she stood taking it all in, she knew this was not the ship. So much had happened since then. She felt changed.

She took her club made of sacred wood, stained with the blood of the island. She stepped out and smashed it down on the Serpunt King's head. It took one stroke, one to slay and the thud was heard. The absence of the king's vocals stopped the warning factions dead. The inhabitants looked up at their fallen king and the charge on the little warrior band was abandoned immediately. The charge for their new target was on. Celine and Daone turned to race past the boulder and further around the mountain.

88. Reacting

Hanuk saw the two women step out from behind the rock. He watched Celine strike the king and the whole energy of the scene changed. His anger at those around him dissipated immediately. The rage he felt was redirected the way of the hill. How dare they! They were no heroes. This was his and the tribe's island. They did not need a saviour and the option to kill the King and reclaim their power had been taken by these intruders. It did not matter that Daone had not swung, she was one of the outside and was not any less immune to the rage instantly built here. The pack moved as one and chased the women. Even the group, cut off, had managed to flank Hanuk from the rear. They all heard and felt the energy shift. A death chase was on.

89. Troubles

Branches of thorns scratched their faces. Their lungs and legs burnt. All they could do was run now. No other option presented itself. They both ran, hearing the sounds of the sea grow nearer. The mountain opened up on the other side to cliffs and the ocean stretched out before them; the place where they had spent so much time, lost in the depths of their own misery. They were out of options as they followed the cliff edge with the sheer rock of the mountain up to the left and the drop of the ocean to their right.

Sea birds flapped out of the way, screeches of annoyance scraping the women's ears. The band of pursuers trod silently and the evidence of their following came in the shrill screams and sssss noises they were so used to hearing now. The cliff banked down in steps all the way to the short beach, becoming more exposed as the tide raced out. Hidden in the rocks, above the tideline, was a small fleet of fishing boats strung out across the cliffs. Fish were suspended on stands, drying. They reached the boats and hastily untied them all. They'd been strung together for safety and to keep them all together in the weather. Once unhooked from the cliff caves they slipped easily down into the water. The two women hurriedly jumped on board and the tide swept in and pulled them out.

They looked back to see the newly united tribe reach the edge themselves. They drew back arms, ready to release spears and projectiles. Hanuk at their lead took a look around and made a definitive noise that neither heard. They braced themselves for the end as they were totally exposed in the boats.

No one fired. They stood and stared. Celine and Daone stared back. The tide was the only loud and moving force. In the distance, the waters of the open ocean swirled and grew in strength. A storm was brewing. The two women floated out, poorly provisioned and bleeding, alone in a sea of troubles.

Acknowledgements

T hank you,

Ellie

William

Craig

Mem

www.ingramcontent.com/pod-product-compliance
Lightning Source LLC
Chambersburg PA
CBHW071148180726
48291CB00007B/2366